VENGEANCE

Justice's Revenge

PAMELA JAMES COLEMAN

S.H.E. PUBLISHING, LLC

VENGEANCE: JUSTICE REVENGE
Copyright © 2024 by Pamela James Coleman

This book is a work of fiction. Names, characters, businesses, organizations, places, events, and incidents either are the product of the author's imagination or are used fictitiously. Any resemblance to actual persons, living or dead, events, or locales is entirely coincidental.

For information contact : Pamela James Coleman
S.H.E. PUBLISHING, LLC (shepublishingllc.com)
www.shepublishingllc.com
info@shepublishingllc.com
Tel: 219.515.8032

ISBN: 978-1-953163-98-1 (*paperback*)

First Edition : March 2024
1 2 3 4 5 6 7 8 9 10

I would like to say Thank you,
to my girls
Rahm Garrett and Leticia Smith
You both got me through a rough time.
You reminded me of who I am and my worth.
I am forever grateful.

TABLE OF CONTENTS

Introduction 1

Chapter 1 – Reya 5

Chapter 2 – Kourtney 37

Chapter 3 – Lyssa 73

Chapter 4 – Harper 99

Chapter 5 – Dina 127

Chapter 6 – We got you! 141

Epilogue 147

INTRODUCTION

"911 - how can I help you?"

"There's a man walking on the highway that looks like he's been in a house fire."

"911 - how can I help you?"

"There's a man walking on Highway 24 he looks drunk and like someone has set him on fire."

Six police cars come speeding down Highway 24 looking for this man. For an hour they searched the area where this man was seen, but nothing. They radioed back if they get another call like that to please get the location that they are calling from, the search continues.

While all of this is going on, Reya is out for her afterwork jog. She jogs every night after work on a well light trail with night. monitors. Reya has moved to the metropolitan area from Hawaii. Reya works at the college campus as a nurse intern, also at the hospital as an on-call emergency nurse intern.

Right before she entered the monitored trail, she noticed feet under a bush, she stopped to check out what was going on. There's a man lying in the shrubs, clothes are burned, his body is charred. Her first reaction was to yell for help. Just as she was about to, he raised his hand to gesture, stop. She leaned in to hear what he was saying.

"Take me...........take me to your house, please!" the man pleaded.

"You need help, you need to go to the hospital." Reya said in a frantic manner.

"NO! take me to your house, I am begging you.!"

Reya helped him up, they walked a block to her apartment. Once in the apartment her nursing instincts kicked in. She placed him in the tub, cut his clothes off and gently cleaned his wounds. She worked with urgency to make sure that he did not go into shock.

Once the wounds were cleaned, she moved him to the sofa, to cover him with blankets. He was starting to shiver, due to lack of clothing. After several glasses of water, and electrolyte drinks, he began talking a little.

She asked what happened to him. With a low raspy voice, he began to tell Reya that he was going around a curve, he pushed the brakes, the car wouldn't. stop. He went off a bridge, was ejected from the car. When the car hit the bottom of the hill it burst into flames, that's how he got the burns.

"I was climbing back to the street when I saw the women from my past and present standing at the top of the hill. At first, I was happy to see them all there, that meant that they still cared about me, right? As I continued back up the ditch," he starts again with the heavy coughing, "I started to think about how I got down here. Are they here to make sure I am, ok? Or are they here to make sure I died? I rolled back down the hill, I crawled into a drain until the police and firefighters left the area."

He is starting to cough more; Reya goes to get him more water.

"We need to call the police to let them know what you think happened so that they can investigate." She remarks.

"No! I will handle this one on my own." He says with firmness.

"I am going to take care of them one at a time!"

"Kourtney"

"Lyssa"

"Harper"

"Dina"

"And you are going to help with each one of them!"

Reya is afraid of him, the way he is talking about taking care of these women. Her voice now shaking as she speaks.

"What do you have planned for them?"

He stares at the ceiling for a few minutes, turns to her with a simple response.

"REVENGE!"

"JUSTICE REVENGE!"

1

REYA

Reya says nothing, except it's time to go to bed. "I must go to work early in the morning. We will talk more about your plan in the morning." That brought Justice's rage down, he agreed to take a break for the night.

It's 6:00am, Reya is at work, her co-workers notice a change in her. They thought it was a good time to talk to her about it. Chantal stopped Reya, "Hey, when is a good time to talk? We are concerned about you."

Reya turned quickly, "Concerned about what? There's nothing to be concerned about."

Reya continued to finish her 12-hour shift. She continued to notice the girls were acting strangely. They were not really talking to her or looking in her direction. She stopped Tasha to ask if everything was okay.

Tasha responded, "We should be asking you that question. You are the one acting differently."

"What do you mean I am acting different," Reya said. "I am fine, just tired from the long days."

Tasha wasn't buying that, "12-hour shift never bothered you before. There were times you would work 12 hours, run 5 miles and party. I don't believe you. Give me a better answer."

Joyce, another co-worker walked over. "Hey, are we finally getting to the bottom of why Reya is acting strange and has a funky attitude?"

Reya looked at both, her voiced now raised, "There is nothing wrong with me, I am fine."

Tasha responded, "Girl, you need to bring that voice level down a bit. You don't talk to us like that, and we are in a hospital."

Chantal walked over, "I heard that over at the nurse's station. OK! So, you are fine, we will drop it. Are we still going to karaoke tonight?"

"Um, I can't tonight."

All three ladies said at the same time, "WHAT! What reason could you possibly have no to go?"

Reya, stumbled to find a quick response, she started with "Um..."

"OH, MY GOODNESS," Chantal yelled, "you have a man, that's it. Now it all makes sense."

Joyce said, "Lower your voice, we are in a hospital, remember?"

Everyone is now staring at Reya; they all agree that she has a man. All her actions say that this is what's going on.

Joyce said, "We need to hear everything about this man. Call him, tell him you will be late tonight."

"Can we do this tomorrow? We have plans for tonight, that is why I can't go tonight. I promise tomorrow night, and the nights on me, OK?"

Reya was now worried how she would explain to Justice, that she was going out? Should she tell the truth or lie? *Why am I so afraid of what he will say or think?* She's afraid, because there is someone living in her house that was planning revenge on four different women, that she was now a part of it. Would she be next?

Reya returns home from work to see Justice who has taken over her office. As she walked in the room, it looked like a war zone. Two of the four walls have been divided into two halves. Each section had a photo of each woman on it. Notes, ideas, and questions for the women.

Justice instructed her to sit down and listen as he began totell her how the plans were going to work. Before he began to speak, Reya asked, "How did you get the photos?"

He responded, "I used your computer to get the needed information." As he explained what he had done, she started yelling at Justice that all of those searches could be tracked back to her. "Are you crazy?" She checked her computer; he had even made folders on her computer desktop.

"Justice these folders can be tracked back to me. Did you ever think about what could happen to me while you carry out your crazy ass plan?" Justice heard the word crazy, he stopped looked at her like he could kill. With a calm voice he told Reya, "You haven't seen crazy. Now sit down and listen to what I have to say."

Reya could feel all the color now leaving her face, her body was starting to get weak. She took a seat to hear what he had to say, to find out how much trouble she was getting herself in. Justice began to explain his thoughts for each woman in detail.

Justice thinks that it will take about three months to gather all the information needed to put his plan into place. "Everything must be perfect," he says. Reya was starting to feel ill; she continued to sit and pay attention. He asked if she was, okay.

"No," Reya responded, "I feel a little queasy, but please continue."

Justice handed her a list of things he needed from the store: rope, lighter, tapc, a gasoline can, and a shovel.

"What, why do you need these things?"

"Don't ask questions just get what on the list. Let's begin by going over the list and how you factor in," he said coolly.

"Kourtney- She is now a manger and owner of an up-scale night club." He has the hours of operation. "She is seeing the security guard that she hired."

Reya looked strange when he handed her another piece of paper at the top it read:

Kourtney- things for Reya to complete.

1) *Follow her for two weeks to learn her routine.*
2) *Have a girl's night out with friends, take photos of the inside doors, how many security people working.*

Reya thought this was good and bad. She would be able to do this list that he had for her and go out with the girls. This would keep everyone happy, except her.

Next on the list was Lyssa.

"Lyssa- she owns six fitness centers, married to a very successful business owner. She is pregnant with twins," He says, "I know I have an order that I wanted to go in. I will not harm her children. We were good friends at one time, I would never want harm to come to her kids."

He hands her another note, this one stating:

1) *Get her routine down.*

2) *You and your friends will start taking classes that she teaches.*

3) *Photos of the inside, this might be harder to do because it is a different atmosphere. All the photos you can take will be helpful.*

"Helpful in what?" Reya asked.

Justice looked at her, this time with a calm expression. "I understand that it is hard to trust me. I need you to do the things that I am asking you to with no more questions. I have no interest in harming you."

Reya agreed that the only questions that she would ask was to clarify his request.

Reya had a question, "The first two plans so far, are similar in action. Is that what you mean to happen?"

"Hey! Thanks for the question, you are paying attention." Reya nodded this time, to keep from getting him upset. She was thinking to herself that she never thought that she would ever be doing something like this. She was still not clear if he is going to harm them or approach them.

He snapped his fingers, "Hey, come back are you okay?"

She thought for a moment, "Yeah, I am ok, it's just," she paused, "are you going to harm them?"

He stared at her. "Again, I will say this, some parts of the plan, you are better off not knowing."

Reya took a deep breath, sat back, and continued to listen to the plan.

"Harper- she is going to be difficult. I have not been able to locate her. It shows that she is in the city somewhere. What she is doing is something that you will have to find out. Lyssa and her are good friends, once you are able to become friends with her then the information needed for Harper should be easy to get."

"Dina- she had a business that failed. She moved in with friends and is now dating a member of a well-known, local church. It is said that she could be pregnant but not confirmed."

Again, he hands her a note. This one stating:

1) *I want you to become a member of the church.*
2) *Always sit near her, after a few trips I need you to start crying.*
3) *She will want to help you, that is the type of person she is.*
4) *Then learn her schedule.*

Reya sat back in disbelief about the plan he has sat in front of her. What's worse was her part in the plan. She could either go along with this plan or call the police.

Reya started a plan of her own. *What if I go to the police? Would they believe I didn't have anything to do with this?*

She had hid this man in her house for a while now, would they ask why she didn't call earlier? With a heavy heart, she convinced herself to help with the plan, the police wouldn't believe her anyway.

Looking over the list of things he wanted her to do, how was she supposed to get this done and work a full-time job? The more she thought about it the more she became ill. This was not the time to get sick. Looking over her list one more time she said, "Let's start with Dina," Reya begins to set his plans into motion.

The very next Sunday Reyna attended church to begin gathering the needed information. Sunday came quick, Reya sat in the back of the church. She heard the pastor say, "All visitors make your way to the front of the church, please."

Reya went to the front of the church, as she was walking to the front she looked around, she saw Dina to her left. Once she was at the front of the church, the pastor asked each person what brought them to the church that day? As Reya stood there, she was thinking to herself that she needed to come up with something fast.

It was now Reya's turn. "Hello, everyone, my name is Reya." She froze as soon as her name left her lips. She said to herself *Oh shit, I said my real name! Oh no! I said shit in the church.* Reya continued; "I have walked by the church several times while services were going on. I would stop to sit on the steps to listen. Today, as I sat on the steps something told me to come inside."

At that moment the church erupted in amens and praise his names. Reya jumped she had never seen reactions like that before in church.

"Things at home are not good," she began to cry. "When things are bad, I will walk past the church, and I begin to feel better." Again, with the amens and praise his names. Reya in turn said, "Amen."

"Thank you for allowing me to attend your church." After she spoke, she returned quickly to her seat. She could see someone heading in her direction. She looked up, it was Dina. She sat down next to Reya.

"Hello, my name is Dina, I want you to know I am here for you. If there is anything that you need, please let me know." Reya asked if they could talk the service was over. Dina agreed.

Once the service was over, they walked outside together, sat on the front steps of the church. They talked for almost an hour, Reya was learning a lot about Dina, as they continued to talk the pastor came outside.

He asked the ladies, "is everything was, okay?" They said, "Yes." He turned to Dina, "Why don't you invite her back to the house. You two can finish your talk there." They both agreed to return to the house to talk. Reya sent Justice a text message, to let him know the progress. He responded, "Thank you for all you are doing."

When they got to the home of the pastor, a Sunday dinner was prepared, and looked tasty. Dina came down the steps with a baby in her arms. The little girl looked like she was three weeks old. Reya remarked how cute the baby was. Dina said, "Thank you."

Suddenly, a look come over Reya's face, Dina asked, "Is everything okay?"

Reya looked down at the ground and then she looked up, "I didn't know that you and the pastor were married."

Dina responded, "No, we are not married yet," with a big smile on her face. "Have a seat Reya let's talk. Like yourself, I met the pastor when I was going through a tough time. I had a business that I was running, that was failing, and I had just lost the love of my life.

"The night that he was in an accident, I was going to tell him that I was pregnant. I had no idea that I was pregnant, when I went to the doctor, they told me that I was five almost six months pregnant. I was feeling okay, I went to the doctor for a regular checkup and that is what they found.

"I got a call that evening, something had happened. There was an accident and I needed to get there quickly. I never got a chance to tell him that I was pregnant." You could see the tears in her eyes as she started to tell the story.

"I became depressed, I had lost everything. I was out walking and came upon the church. Sitting on the steps of the church when the pastor came outside, and the rest is what you see today. Let's change the subject." And Reya agreed.

"Would you like to stay here awhile, so that you can work out what is going on at home?"

Reya said she would love to come back to talk to her. Dina was happy to hear that Reya wanted to come back.

"Let me get you my schedule so that you can find me when you need me."

Reya said to herself, *it can't be this easy. I hope the others are this easy.*

Days turned into weeks; weeks turned into months. During this time Reya was working hard on keeping her end of the deal. While she was working on this list for Justice, she was starting to change.

Soon, Reya stopped keeping in touch with her family and her usual girls' nights were starting to disappear. She spent all her time working on the things that Justice needed. After work she would go home or work on the plans he had on the wall.

One day, it was time to head to Kourtney's club. Reya thought this would be a good time to keep the girls happy and work on this dam list. She asked Chantal, Tasha, and Joyce if they would like to go to a new club that she had heard about.

The ladies loved the idea, it was even better because it came from Reya. The ladies started asking questions, "did you leave the man?" "Are you okay?" "Did he do anything to you?"

"NOTHING Ladies, I just want to go out and have some fun with my girls for a change. Let's just get dressed up and go out, drinks on me tonight." They all cheered, set a time for later tonight. They all went back to work.

Once she was home, she informed Justice of how she has her plan set up for tonight, he agreed and said she was doing a good job.

When they arrived at the club, the music was great, and the atmosphere was upscale. Each table was separated by a very nice partition to provide privacy. The ladies were the first ones to get to the club, this allowed Reya to take clear photos.

As Reya walked through the club taking photos, she was acting like she was taking selfies. As the people started to come into the club, they would jump into her photos. With others getting in her photos, it made it look normal with her taking the photos.

Reya was able to get photos of the doors, the exits and the security personnel. It was time for the ladies to hit the floor. They danced the night away. A couple of gentlemen sent rounds of drinks to the table. That night was one of the best nights they had had in a while.

The ladies were on the dance floor when they noticed that one of ladies was missing. Reya began to panic. The first thing that came to mind was Justice had something to do with Joyce disappearance. There was familiar laughter coming from a table in the back of the club.

Heading in that direction, as they got closer, the ladies saw Joyce. She had found herself a young gentleman and retreated to the back of the club for privacy. Joyce assured them she was okay and that they should go back to dancing.

Back to dancing they went, before they realized it was 3:00 am, the club was closing. They were the first ones into the club and the last one's out. Now in the parking lot, Chantal, wanted to know when they were coming back. Tasha agreed; Joyce was a few rows over exchanging phone numbers with the young man.

Reya responded that it would be great to come back, "but I have something else that would be just as fun."

"We are all ears," Tasha said.

"I have found a place to work out that sounds great. Maybe we could…"

Before she could finish Chantal said, "Who are you calling fat?"

Reya said, "You didn't let me finish, we could take yoga or a meditation class to help with the stress of work. Now Chantal, that was what I was trying to say… Geez," stated Reya.

"My apologies," Chantal said.

"We can talk about a date that will work well for us all to check this place out. I promise we will return to this club."

With mumbled voices, "Do any of you need a rideshare called?"

Everyone was okay, including Joyce who was leaving with the young man she just met. Joyce dropped her location in everyone's phone so that they could see where she was always located.

Once home, she uploaded the photos from her phone to share with Justice. Just as the photos completed the upload, in walked Justice with a sleepy look on his face. "So how did it go," he asked?

"I think it went well," Reya said, "it was a win-win. You were correct, I was able to get photos for you and go out with the ladies to keep the questions at bay!"

Justice began to hang the photos under Kourtney's photo. Reya slipped out of the room while he was working on that. It was now 4:00 am, she had to be at work by 6:00 am all she wants if a 30-minute power nap. She stopped at the sofa, to lay her head down. Justice came over with blankets and covers her and set a timer to go off in a half an hour.

While she was asleep, he went into the kitchen, to prepare her an on-the-go breakfast, coffee and pack her lunch. As the breakfast was on the stove, he slipped into her bathroom to start her shower, and lay her clothes on the bed for her. The alarm was ringing in the living room, and Reya started to move around.

"What's that smell?" She yelled and walked into her bedroom to see Justice had her shower going and coffee waiting for her on the sink.

She said, "Thank you," and he left her room, shutting the door behind him. While she was getting ready, Justice packed her bag with breakfast and lunch. Reya was now dressed and ready to go.

"Here you go," Justice said. "A large cup of coffee to get you through the day, breakfast, and lunch so you can take a nap at work and not go out to find lunch. Thank you for everything you did last night."

He headed to the back bedroom and shut the door while Reya was still standing there shocked. Her phone rang, it was her parents, she knew she needed to take the call. They called all last night while she was at the club.

It had been months since she had contact with her parents like she used to. She still sent a text message twice a week, so that they would know that she was okay. Reya knew that if she FaceTimed with them, her parents would pick up instantly that there was a problem.

So, she sends a quick text, "Hey guys, I was out with the girls late last night, that why I didn't pick up and I am running out the door now to catch the bus. Can we talk later?"

Nothing came back, Reya ran out the door to catch the bus. Once she arrived at work. All the ladies looked like they had been out way too late last night. The only one that looked refreshed was Joyce, and she was not giving any details on what happened to her last night.

Reya suggested they rest for that and they could work out the next day. Again, Reya's phone buzzed, it was her parents with an ultimatum, if they did not FaceTime or hear her voice in the next 48 hours, they were flying in. She responded quickly, "Yes sir, yes ma'am, I will call in the next day or so."

Two days later, the ladies are rested, dressed to workout standing in front of a new facility. Tasha asked, "How you keep finding these new places? It's so nice to have the old Reya back. We are so sorry that things didn't work out between you and the guy."

Reya with a strange look on her face. "Who says we are not working out?" followed by a wink.

The doors opened and there stood Lyssa. She was a very beautiful pregnant woman. Reya's crew was already whining about exercising. Lyssa assured them, when class was over other than seeing the sweat on their clothes, they wouldn't know that they had done a workout.

The whining continued. Now down on their mats, the ladies sat with legs crossed. Starting with deep breathing in and out. Then some hard stretches.

"We are all going to sit on our mats, legs straight lean back as far as you can go for 30 seconds."

Oh! I can feel this Reya said to herself.

"Roll over let's go into a plank position for a minute." There was a loud thump, Joyce had toppled over and all the girls began to laugh with her, not at her. The workout continued for another 30 more minutes before there was a break.

Lyssa also felt a connection to the ladies, which made the class go smoothly. During the break they walked around looking at the photos, awards, and wedding photos that she had on the walls. There she was Harper, hanging on the wall. Reya pointed to the photo, "Who is the lady that you are with? she looks so familiar."

"That is my friend Harper St. James. She is an author; she has now joined the academy to become a private investigator. After a friend of ours vanished in an accident, with no answers as to what happened to him. She doesn't want others to feel that pain. It has been months; we still have no answers."

"What happened?" Reya asked.

"Our mutual friend was involved in what seemed to be a bad accident. When his friends arrived at the scene, the car was in flames. The flames were so high they could almost reach us at the top of the ridge. Once the flames were extinguished, we all waited for the bad news.

"That's when the fire teams called the police down to the car. He was gone."

Reya jumped in shock, "what really, he was gone?"

"Yes gone, so much time has gone by that we doubt if we will ever get any answers." Lyssa turned to Reya, "You know, I forgot that Harper will be stopping by this evening. She comes by once a week to make sure me and the twins are doing okay. You can meet her I think you and your friends will all get along."

Reya was surprised, she would be able to meet and talk to Harper. This may be the chance she can get the information on both ladies at one time. The door buzzed and in walked a young lady with poise and a business style. Reya was confused, wait if she is in the academy, why is she not dressed in a uniform?

Harper laughed as she stood there looking like she had just left the fashion show runway. Red business suit, black cami, black, red bottoms, with a matching briefcase. Lyssa begins the introduction of the ladies.

"Harper and I are going out to dinner would you ladies like to join?" They all said yes but were concerned about what they had on.

Lyssa said they would keep it casual and comfortable. The only one in this group that would look out of place was Harper, and she was used to that. They all laughed. Reya sent Justice a text to let him know what was happening. To her surprise, his response was "Great! But then her phone rang, and Justice was on the line and immediately started with, "But, we or you have a problem."

"What problem do I have?" Reya responded.

"Your parents are in town, they have called your apartment, as well as coming over here knocking on the door. When no one answered the door, a note came under the door. It said, 'we are here to see you, call us immediately or we are returning with the police.'"

In a stern voice, Justice told her to handle it. "Call them while you are out to dinner, so that they can hear your voice. Calm them down and keep them from this house." Reya agreed that she needed to keep them away from the house. If not for their own safety but for hers.

During dinner Reya was able to get more information than Justice wanted. Lyssa and Harper became friends through an issue with Justice. They didn't want to talk about it, they were happy that they had each other to get through it.

Lyssa was a world-renowned fitness instructor, pregnant with twins, and married to a wealthy businessman. She lived in a beautiful home in the Burbs. She was currently working on opening more exercise studios. She was really going places.

Harper had released a book; she joined the police academy to become a detective. Her goal was to help solve cases that have to do with domestic issues. Her main goal was to solve what happened to Justice.

Over the next few months, she would have a few local book events. She invited all of the ladies to join her, "it should be a good time," Harper said.

Reya excused herself, said she had to make a phone call to her parents who have been calling her all afternoon. She reached her parents, who began with nothing but questions. "Where are you? Are you ok? Why hadn't you called us?"

Once Reya was able to get them to stop talking, she suggested that they meet for dinner. They set a time and place, with that done it seemed to calm her parents down, everyone was happy.

She returned to the group to finish out the evening. Before the ladies separated for the night, Harper shared the locations of her events. They all exchanged numbers, so that they could set another outing together. Once home, Reya was extremely tired, she asked Justice if they could go over the information the next day. She didn't have to go to work, and they would have all day. He agreed.

Justice let Reya sleep in, she had been working hard to help him, that was the least he could do. While she slept, he cleaned up the apartment, fed her animals and prepared lunch, since she had slept through breakfast.

Once awake, Reya was able to update Justice on both women. He was very excited about the amount of detailed information she was able to collect in just one night. While they talked, Justice said, "I have something for you." Her heart began to beat quickly, scared of what he was going to do.

He reached under the desk, rattling a bag as he sat up. She dropped to the floor and screamed "DON'T SHOOT ME!".

He looked at her with concern. "Why would I shoot you?"

"You are planning to hurt these women. What if I stop helping, are you going to hurt me too?"

He sat there and said nothing. After a few minutes, he asked, "Really? Is that what you think?"

Reya responded, "You have these plans."

"Yes, I do have plans, but did I ever say that I was going to hurt them? Did I ever say or show signs that I would hurt you?"

Reya stopped, she sat back in the chair, and a calm came over her. "No! you never said anything about hurting them. You have only been nice to me, when you raise your voice, I get nervous and scared a little bit. The detailed plans that you are getting for these women. I thought that you were......." she stopped.

"That is correct... YOU *thought*. I never said what I was going to do, I want to seek revenge and how that looks has not come together yet. So will you accept this gift, please"

Reya reached out for the gift bag. As she began to open the bag a small smile came over her face. "Are you going to stare in the bag or take the stuff out?"

Reya pulled out a new running outfit with matching sneakers. For him to get the things that she really liked made her smile. Reya apologized for thinking so badly of him. Justice accepted her apology, he suggested that they take a break, and cook dinner. Once dinner was done, the two went back to the office.

Looking at all four on the wall, adding notes and clarifying that he had all of it correctly placed. They both sat back to look at the wall. Reya looked at the wall, Lyssa had set days and times for her classes she was a month away from her due date. Harper had shared her event dates. Dina had nothing really going on but church, we know when and where that took place. Also, the address to her home. Kourtney's schedule was a little over the place, yet still easily able to track.

As they confirmed with each other and started to walk away from the office. There was a loud banging on the door. It was her parents. She missed their dinner appointment. Now they are on the other side of her door. "If you don't open this door, we are calling 911."

Reya tries to calm them down through the door. She asked them to please return to the restaurant, she would meet them there in 20 minutes. Her parents refused; they wanted her to open the door. They gave her five minutes to do so. If not, they would call the police, and would not leave until the police arrived.

She asked if they would trust her, and go to the restaurant, she would meet them there. Her dad refused, he started to ram into the door to open it. Her mom was pleading with her to open the door. Then, her dad stopped hitting the door, when he turned there stood the police. One of the neighbors had called the police to report a disturbance.

Reya's parents explained that their daughter lived here, she had been acting strange. She stopped keeping in touch with them and now they were here for her from Hawaii, but she refused to open the door. After hearing the story, the police asked Reya to open the door. She looked at Justice and nodded.

Reya cracked open the door, she agreed to open the door for the police only. She wanted her parents to stay in the hallway while she talked to them. Her parents were devastated. Once inside, one of the officers asked Reya what was going on. While the other officer walked through the apartment. While walking around the apartment, the officer stopped at the office with all the plans on the wall.

He turned to Reya, "What's happening in here?"

For a moment she thought, *is this a good time to say what's going on?* They would take him out of the apartment, and she would be free.

Quick with her response, "Nothing much, I have four friends, whose birthday are all in the same month. I am trying to figure out their schedules to plan a surprise party for them."

Both officers laughed and responded, "Okay. You have a lot of detailed information; this should be a good party. At first, I thought you were planning a kidnapping."

Reya laughed; "I am too small to do a thing like that."

"Ms. Kapono, why are your parents so upset?"

"I have gotten so pre-occupied with work and friends, that I didn't realize that so much time had gone by without talking to them. I used to talk to them daily, and I was having fun with friends, working out and working, that time just got away from me. Days became weeks, weeks turned into months. I tried to make it better by setting up a dinner with them, I was running late. They just took things in their own hands. Now we are here."

The police officer asked her what she would like for them to do.

"Can you please tell them I will meet them at the same restaurant, same time, in two days. I don't want to talk to them after the way they have acted. I will call them in the morning to talk through this with them."

The officers agreed that this is not the best time for them to talk face-to-face. "You both need time to calm down."

Reya thanked the police officers for their help. She opened the door to let them out, her parents started to rush the door. One of the officers gestured to them to stop. "This is not a good time for you guys to talk. You both need a cooling off period, let's talk outside."

Reya closed the door behind them, Justice told her she did a good job. She fell to the floor in tears. "I am exhausted, I don't know how much more of this I can take." Justice suggested that she goes for a jog, to help calm her down. She agreed with him, she watched her parents leave with tears in her eyes. Wondering if what she was doing was the right thing.

She got ready to go out for a while to clear her mind. She usually run five to eight miles a day. She needed some time to herself thinking ten to twelve today would be what she needed to relax. When she left for her jog, Justice slipped out of the apartment. As he was checking to make sure the hallway was clear, Frankie slipped out without him noticing.

Reya returned from her job, she noticed that Frankie didn't greet her at the door like normal. She walked through the apartment looking for him and noticed Justice was missing also. Panic started to set in, the door open it was Justice.

Then she turned around and saw that he stood in the doorway covered in dirt and breathing heavy.

"Are you ok?" Reya asked. "Where have you been? Where's Frankie? Did anyone see you?"

Justice face became enraged, "Why are you asking all these damn questions? Yes, I am ok! I was hiding from the neighbors, it's none of your business where I have been. I don't give two shits about Frankie he's your problem not mine."

Reya was angry at the way he replied to her but she refused to let him know that he had made her angry. Justice took a shower and laid down on the sofa. He looked at Reya, he saw a look on her face he hadn't seen before. "I am sorry for the way I talked to you; I have a lot on my mind and all these questions are not helping."

Reya turned to him and spat, "You have a lot on your mind!? You are not the one who must stalk people, lie to her family and friends, not to mention the Police. If anyone should be yelling at someone it should be me!" Reya threw her hands up, "I can't deal with this anymore tonight."

It was morning, the only thing that helped Reya clear her mind was going for another jog. She realized that she couldn't go into work with the mindset that she was in. Ginger needed to go out, they both could us the run. Five miles later with an exhausted Ginger they headed back to the apartment.

Reya was now relaxed from all the drama of yesterday, she could get ready to go to work without the girls thinking something was wrong. As she approached the apartment, she glanced behind the apartment building. She saw four holes, she paused to get a closer look.

She stood there for a few minutes in shock. These holes looked like graves, Oh no! Is this what Justice was doing? Is this why he was dirty? Ginger started barking, Reya jumped, she picked up Ginger and ran into the building. She was quickly at her apartment, struggling to find her keys.

She heard footsteps behind her. When she turned to see if there was someone behind her, Reya screamed "Why are you doing this?"

She began to yell for help. Doors started to open, Reya drops Ginger. Neighbors were coming out in the hallway, to see why Reya is yelling. They were all looking at each other with a puzzled look. Ginger was there running around in circles. In front of her apartment door was a small SUV on fire. Reya was gone.

POLICE SUMMARY REPORT

The police arrived at Reya's apartment, there was chaos everywhere. They immediately called for back-up to control the crowd. Three police cars later, the officers had the hallway cleared. Now to focus on the neighbors who could help with the issue at hand.

Apartment 3A shared his story of a strange man that came in and out of Reya's apartment all hours of the night. When he saw this person, they were always wearing black. He started seeing him hanging around the hallways about five or six months ago. It may have been longer.

Apartment 3D told the police of the same person digging holes in the back of the apartment building. She didn't think anything of it. She thought that Reya had gotten permission to plant a garden. When she looked out the window this morning, those holes didn't look like a garden.

Apartment 3G informed the police of loud conversations that came from Reya's apartment. The conversations were loud enough that she thought that she may be in danger. Then she would see Reya the next morning and she was fine. She stopped her to make sure that she was okay, because of the noise. She always apologized and said that it was just a disagreement, and the man would never hurt her.

While conducting the interviews and waiting for the keys to Reya's apartment, Reya's parents. Before they could ask what was going on, the questions turned to them.

"You were here the other night to see your daughter and an argument broke out; can you all tell me more about that night?"

Her parents began with how it had been months since their daughter had consistent conversations with them. They used to talk to her every day, then it went to once every two weeks. They flew in from Hawaii to see what was going on and why they had lost contact with her. Officer Hill asked if they could tell them more about her boyfriend.

At the same time her parents said "What? There's no boyfriend. She has never spoken of anyone." Officer Hill explained that the neighbors have seen a male coming and going from her apartment. They started to see this person leaving her place a few months ago.

"It might have been the same time that she started to lose contact with you all."

Finally, the property owner arrived with the key. The officers, property owner and her parents entered the apartment. Officer Bates asked everyone to be careful when they walked past the little SUV, that was evidence, they didn't want that disturbed.

Officer Hill asked everyone to stand at the door for a moment while they walked around. They didn't want anything tampered with. As the officers walked through the apartment, they both stopped at Reya's office. Officer Bates asked the parents if anything look different to them.

Reya's mom said the home had a strange smell to it. It didn't have the floral smell that she usually kept in her apartment. Her mom also pointed out there were men's clothes laying at the end of the sofa she had never seen before. Everything else looked normal to her.

Officer Bates replied, "Thank you, if it is not too much trouble can you both come this way, I need you to look in this room for us."

Everyone was now in the room and the questioning started with the owner. "When was the last time you were in this apartment?"

He thought for a minute, "It has been about six months since I came here to do routine check-ups, she said everything was okay. I didn't think anything of it. I have a lot of tenants who ask that I don't stop by unless they call me."

Now it's the parents turn, "Can you look at the wall? Do you know these ladies? The way the photos are displayed it looks like a war room."

At that time an officer walked past, and he stopped at the room. "Oh, we were here the other day, she said that they are her friends, she was planning a birthday party for them that is why this is set up this way."

Everyone stopped, Officer Bates looked at him, "Did you hear what you just said?" The other officer stood there looking stupid. "I guess when you say it out loud it does sound stupid. Okay Sherlock, then who are the women then if they are not her friends."

Her parents said that they didn't know who these women were. Reya had three friends that work with her and none of them look like these women.

Now the officers were confused, "Why would she have this up here? Who does the male clothes belong to? We need to talk to her friends to see if they know who these people are."

An officer ran into the apartment, "You need to come downstairs quickly." Everyone ran down the stairs to see what was so urgent. When they got downstairs, everyone stopped.

"What the hell is this?" There were four holes that looked like graves, and then there was one started but not completed. What they couldn't understand was why each one have a letter on it?

The letters were R, K, L, H and D what did that mean? Why were they here?

2
KOURTNEY

"Why did this have to happen? There was nothing we hadn't gone through that we didn't or couldn't work out, now he's gone."

Ty, her longtime friend, sat there with her. He was there to listen to her and give support during this time of confusion.

"You need to calm down, take a deep breath so that I can understand what you are trying to tell me."

Kourtney took a deep breath, stared out the window, and turned to him to begin her story. "I was leaving work, my phone rang telling me I need to get to Jensen Road because there was an accident. The only thing I could think of was whether it was my mom or my dad. I didn't know what was going on. When I arrived there, they were those people associated with Justice standing on the edge of the road looking down at flames coming from the bottom."

Ty asked, "Why were you all there?"

She continued, "When I looked down at the flames, I saw his car on fire."

Ty yelled "Oh my Goodness where was he?"

"They used that the thing to put the car flames out, but when they did, was nowhere to be found."

At this point Ty stood, "What do you mean he was nowhere to be found? Did you see him leave?"

"No! The flames were bad; you could barely see the rescue team. Everyone looked confused, no one knew what happened to him. They told us all to go home. If they got any information that they would contact his family and they could tell us what is going on."

Ty gave her a hug, "You need to get some rest. Maybe tomorrow when you are rested, you may hear something, if not maybe working on your business will help you take your mind off this for a little while."

She told him, "I'm now in the right frame of mind to think about the business right now."

Ty said, "I need you to relax, I'll be back in a few days to check on you." Before leaving he made sure she took a hot shower, put on fresh clothes, and had food in her home to eat until he returned. Kourtney grabbed a blanket, and she laid down on the sofa.

Ty returned a few days later, Kourtney was still on the sofa, it looked as if she only moved when she needed to go to the bathroom. She was still in the same clothes that he left her in and the home had a bad odor on it. Ty wanted to yell at her, but he knew that she was in pain, so he encouraged her again to shower. While she was in the shower he opened the windows, threw out all the bad food and started cooking meals for her to eat on.

TY called her mother for help. At one point, they thought she needed to go to the hospital to talk to someone. After a shower, her mother sat her down to eat some of the food that Ty made for her. As she ate her food and talked to her mother and Ty, she started to feel better. Ty and her mother cleaned her apartment, washed her clothes, things seem to show signs of returning to normal.

Ty looked into the living room and there he saw Kourtney and her mother dancing; it brought a smile to his face. They both joined Ty in the dining room, where he had papers on the table. He had picked up school information to bring to her to look over. She nodded her head that she was ready to hear what he had found for her.

"I found a couple of S3 month courses you can take. One is in Management; the other is in Business education."

She asked in a low voice, "Can I take both?"

Ty responded, "Of course you can take both. I will make a deal with you, if you want to take these classes, you will not go alone. I will take them with you." She was very excited and instantly responded, "Sign me up!"

For the next three months they went to class together, with each day that passed, Kourtney was improving. She seemed stronger and focused on her classes and what she could do with her new education and certification.

She thought to herself that she always wanted to have a business that would offer dance classes to the community. To be an instructor as well as a business owner would be an amazing accomplishment. One afternoon as Kourtney was walking home, she saw a building that would be perfect for what she had in mind for the community.

She took down the information that was posted on the door to contact the owners to see the inside and what she would need to do to make the purchase of the building.

When Ty arrived at the apartment, she told him what she wanted to do and about the building that was for sale. Ty flashed a big smile, asked her what he needed to do to help her get this done.

"Right now, I just want to contact the owners to see the inside to make sure that it will work for what I want it to do."

The next day she called the owners to set up a meeting. The owners would meet with her in the next two days, they were interested in hearing her vision for the building. During the two-day wait, Ty helped her prepare for a business plan on what she planned to do with the building and how it would impact the community.

It was time for the meeting, Ty went with Kourtney for support, while waiting for the owner of the building to arrive her leg began to shake. Ty grabbed her hand, told her to relax because she had this. She was about to respond to him with a thank you when the doors opened, and it was the owner.

"Thank you for being prompt to our meeting, I would like to hear your vision for this warehouse."

"I would like to bring dance back to the neighborhood, I would like for it to be a safe place for students to practice cheer and dance. I would like to offer couples classes, as well as classes just for fun."

"I am selling this building for $150,000; this building has been in my family for over 100 years. My wife and I do not have children to pass this down to, that is why we have been very selective on who we sell to and need to know what they intent was for this property. I am going to put a few serious stipulations on the sale of this property. You will need to complete both of your classes and show me or my wife your certifications. You have six months to pay the entire $150,000 before you can take possession of the building. Or pay us $75,000 in three months and show proof that the balance has been financed by the bank of our picking."

Kourtney agreed to the stipulations, and they shook hands. He said the only reason he was taking a chance on her was because her plans were for the community. As soon as she was outside, she and Ty jumped in joy that one of the biggest steps towards her business is coming true.

"Let's meet after class tomorrow to get a plan together on how to raise the money needed to buy this building." Kourtney had a few weeks left of classes. During that time, she focused on getting her certificates. Once she got those it was nothing but fundraising for the next three months.

With certificates in hand, she proudly took them to Mr. and Mrs. Bridges, they both were very proud of what she had accomplished. She shared her fundraising plans with them. Until the Bridges felt comfortable with her, she was unable to go inside of the building.

On Saturday and Sunday afternoons, the local high schools would use the parking lot for practice. She would teach classes Tuesday, Wednesday, and Thursday. Saturday morning, she would host the high school step competitions. "What kind of classes are you going to teach?" Mrs. Bridges asked.

The classes she would teach would be a sample of what was to come when/if she got the building.

When she first started the classes, she had ten people in attendance, mostly friends and family. That number quickly grew to 30 people for all three days. It was going great. Yet Kourtney wasn't sure that she was doing enough to raise money. Kourtney added events to the Saturday line-up, the parking lot was large enough to also host local yard sales. To rent a table they would pay 10% of sales, this way no one would go home without any profit. If they didn't have a good day of sales, they could home without losing money.

The neighborhood was excited about the attention and foot traffic that they were getting. The Saturday activities brought in more funds than her classes. Kourtney moved one of her classes to Saturday morning to get more exposure to what is coming to the neighborhood.

As Saturday was ending one of the ladies from her class stopped to ask her what she was doing with the parking lot on Sunday morning.

Kourtney responded, "It is not being used during that time, why do you ask?"

"My church has been looking for a place to hold outside services while the church undergoes a few repairs. Would you be open to letting us use the space for 10% of the Sunday offerings?"

"I would love to help the church, there's no need to pay to I am more than happy to help." She worked with Ty, to make sure that everything they needed to have church on Sunday was in the storage shed.

When people heard about church in nature for the next five Sundays, people came from miles away to join. Special guest speakers were invited, people walking by stopped in to hear the service. Ty had a table set up outside the gate to give information about the business to come. She didn't want to set it up inside to take away from the amazing service that was taking place inside.

On any given Sunday, service would last two hours. As service was ending, the preacher asked Kourtney to join them at the front of the congregation. As she walked to the front people were smiling at her, not sure why they were smiling but she smiled back and continued to walk to the front.

Once she reached the preacher, he grabbed both of her hands, he began to pray with her and for her. Once he stopped, he thanked her for allowing them to use the parking lot.

The preacher gestured to one of the deacons to bring up a box to the stage. "Kourtney," he began, "we all know what you are trying to bring to the community. It's been a long time since we had anyone pour into the community like you have. With that being said, we would like to present you with the offerings from today's service.

"In this box we have raised $7,835.00 to go towards the amount needed to purchase the warehouse."

Kourtney was overwhelmed by the gesture, she became faint. Someone saw her starting to fall and ran to the front with a chair for her to sit down.

Kourtney composed herself and stood to thank everyone that was there, and everyone that contributed to the fundraising. She promised that she would do her best to stay true to the vision for the community.

Riding home she began to think of additional ways to use the building that would continue to respect the goal and donations from the church.

"What about a night club?"

Ty shook his head, "How would you explain a night club, using church money?"

When she reached her apartment, she had a plan. "Sit down Ty, listen to this. The money that the church gave would be for the rooms that the exercise classes will take place. The bingo games for the elderly and family fun night. Those rooms will have dedicated by the church.

"When people come in, they will see that the funds raised by the church was spent on those rooms. That will remove all and any connections to the nightclub. The night club would run at respectable time. Friday night 7pm- midnight old school music with no alcohol being served. Still respecting the church's donations. Saturday night would be ladies' night with male dancers. Not striping just dancing, the age has to be 25 year of age and older.

"If we keep the age limit to 25 years and older that will keep the chance of a fight to a minimum. That's it!" Kourtney yelled, "it can be done, and no one will get hurt. I would also need to have an entrance made so that the two business do not encounter each other. All we need now is a name for the club, what do you have in mind Ty?"

"Let me think on it," he replied, "I will have one for you before it is time to open. You know tomorrow you are a few days away from the 3-month mark what are you going to do?"

"I am going to make an appointment with the bank to deposit this money and see where we are and what are our options going forward."

Ty gave her a hug, he said that he was glad she was doing better, he was worried about her. To see her this happy was good for his soul. She responded "Thank you for not giving up on me. Your friendship means the world to me."

Kourtney woke up, the first thing she did was call the bank.

"Hello Kourtney, how is everything going? How can I help you?"

"I would like to make an appointment, to deposit a check and to see what the status of my fundraising," she replied.

"You are in luck," the teller said. "I have a cancellation, are you able to get here within an hour?"

"Yes," Kourtney said, "I will be right there." As she ran out the door she sent Ty a text, "I have an appointment in less than 30 minutes. Stay by your phone."

"Good luck!" came back from Ty.

Kourtney made it to the bank with fifteen minutes to spare, this gave her time to pull herself together and to prepare for all scenarios that the teller could share with her.

The teller escorted her to her desk, "How have you been? It looks like things are going really well with your goals to purchase the warehouse."

"It is," Kourtney replied.

"Yes, let me see the deposit that you have there, and I can give you a current update." As Kourtney sat nervously, the teller turned to her, "I have some very good news for you."

"I am all ears," Kourtney said.

"Well, as of this moment you have $183,626.82 in your account."

"Wait, what?" Kourtney said.

"Yes, at your three-month mark you have over what you need to purchase the building, without any additional financial needs."

Kourtney sat there for a little bit, then she asked, "My I use your phone? I would like to call Mr. and Mrs. Bridges to let them know where we are on the money."

The teller stepped away from the desk so that Kourtney could make the call.

"Hello Mr. and Mrs. Bridges?"

"Yes, dear how can we help you?" asked Mrs. Bridges.

"I have all of the money raised as of today, how would you like to proceed with the sale of the property?"

"That is amazing, we are very proud of you and what you have done to reach this point in making your visions come true. I will reach out to our real estate agent to let them know we are ready to sell. Just one last thing that we need you to do before we make the final exchange."

"Yes ma'am, what is it that you would like me to do?"

"We need you to go downtown and secure all the permits that you will need to run the business that you want to run. I also need you to have insurance on the property before it exchanges hands. We will have the contracts ready for you to sign in three weeks. That will give you the 21 days needed to get the permits and insurance required to take over the building."

With the extra money, she wanted to decorate the warehouse from the inside out. Plant shrubs outside to make it more inviting for clients to come into the building. Kourtney continued to do her fundraising, she wanted to make sure that everything was covered, her employees, things needed for the building. She wanted everything to be perfect.

Before she would see the Bridges to sign the paperwork, she wanted to meet with them and the church preacher to share what the schedule would like. She will conveniently leave out the plan to open a night club.

On Sundays the club would be closed, this would make it available to the church who needed to use it at no charge.

Monday-Wednesday- classes would be taught throughout the day. Dance classes, health, and fitness classes. Cheer classes with the high school students. She would also like to add a salsa class for couples. She wanted everyone to feel good about themselves and know their self-worth.

On Thursdays it would rotate between bingo and spoken word/open mic night. This would provide a platform for local artists to be seen. Her plan was to invite producers to view the artists, for each artist that signed a contract she would get paid $1,000.00.

On Fridays those who were 25 and older would be allowed to attend with old school music and no alcohol served from seven to midnight.

On Saturdays it would be ladies' night only, with professional dancers on an up-scale classy club. With no back-room visits.

Kourtney was set to meet with the owners to buy the warehouse. She had the insurance papers, permits along with the schedule and drawing to show how she wanted the inside to look.

"Everything looks great," said Mr. Bridges, "the building is yours."

They exchanged paperwork, keys, and hugs.

"One last thing, would you like to attend the ribbon cutting ceremony? I would love for you to be my honored guest and I have a surprise for you."

"How can we say no? We look forward to attending your event." Kourtney called Ty to share her vision, he was on it, she also asked, "Starting today would you like to be my personal assistant? With pay of course."

Ty laughed and said, "I thought I was just with no pay. I would be more than happy to help you."

"Great I will plan the ribbon cutting ceremony for two months out that will give me time to get the warehouse just how we visioned it."

After she hung up with Ty, she started calling local contractors for quotes. Later that afternoon, she found one that could do what she wanted while staying in her budget. The last thing she needed was for the surprise for the Bridges. *Who can make this sign that I need.* Reaching out to the contractor he was able to reach out to the person who needed to make the sign.

She was going to name her space "The Bridges Community & Wholeness Center." She was very proud of the choice that she made, also hoping that Mr. & Mrs. Bridges would be happy also. Her plan was to keep the family connected to the building as much as possible. Everything was going well; the rooms were set up to accommodate all of her classes.

One of the hallways that was dedicated to bingo, yoga, and meditation was dedicated to the church. Kourtney's plan was to thank everyone that helped to support the vision somewhere in the building.

They were now a few days from the ribbon-cutting event, the outside looked amazing, she had the parking lot re-paved, shrubs and flowers outlined the building to make it feel inviting.

It was the day of the ceremony, everyone was there, the people that helped raise the money, the church, the Bridges, and the local news. She stood before the crowd very nervously; she began to speak. "Thank you all for coming, thank you all for your support of my dream. Today is special in so many ways, in addition to welcoming you to my new business, I would like to share the name of it, I would like to welcome you all to 'The Bridges Community & Wholeness Center.'"

The banner dropped revealing the sign. Also on the sign were photos of the Bridges and all past Bridges that own the building. Mrs. Bridges was unable to contain her emotions.

She asked them to join her at the podium, she asked them to grab the scissors with her and to open the facility. The crowd cheered as they cut the ribbon, everyone was surprised how she had turned a warehouse into a beautiful place. There was everything from things for kids to do, to the seniors that can come to the building. As the night closed, when Kourtney opened the donation box, she began to count the money left in the box, there was well over $8,000.00. She was beyond happy this would be set aside to pay Ty for four months, while they got the business up and running.

A week later classes started, instead of paying the instructors, they would keep all their payments except for the 10% which came to her for the use of the space. Now that the community side of the building was up and running, it was time to work on the club. The name of the club was "Unique."

She sat down with her business manager to see what the best options were to handle the club side of things. They planned another ribbon cutting for the next Friday night. What was not known, while she put together the community center the club side of things had been put together also.

The plan was to operate the club on Friday and Saturday nights. No one could purchase a ticket at the door, ticket sales were cut off at noon on Thursdays. If any of the church members had questions when or if they heard about the club running out of the same building, she would be prepared to show why this club was also good for the community.

Saturday night's ribbon cutting ceremony for the club went well. Everyone who attended had an amazing time. The happiness was short lived, as Kourtney approached the front door, there they were. The church board was there waiting for her. She greeted them with a smile, told them how happy she was to see. "Are you all here to take a class?"

One of the older members yelled, "No! we are here to talk to you about this blasphemy that is taking place in this building, that the money we raised to help open."

"Yes ma'am, please come in and let's chat."

"As she was showing the member to the conference room, Ty came into the building. Kourtney turned to him, "Can you please bring in a tray for our guest?"

"Not a problem," he responded to her.

"We need you to stop this and stop it now."

"I understand your concerns about this. I am pleased to say to you that this is for ladies over 25, and there is no alcohol on the premises. It is set up to be a safe place that ladies can go out and have clean fun."

"What about the dancers?" One said.

"The dancers are covered below the waist area. It is an illusion for the ladies no more no less."

You could tell they began to ease. "If I can't tell my mother about it, then it will not happen in this building." After an hour of conversation and tea everyone separated with a better understanding of what is taking place in the building. Everything was going great, classes were packed, the bingo game for the seniors was a hit. The club was running smoothly. Kourtney felt as if nothing could go wrong.

But that was soon to change. The newness of the community center was starting to wear off, and the income that was once steady was slowing. The club was the only part of the business that stayed consistent. Kourtney was concerned about how she was going to keep the center open and pay her employees. What could she do with the club that was generating an extreme amount of money? She thought to herself, *I am going to leave things alone, everything will work out., it has too.*

One Saturday night at the club, Kourtney was approached by a lady. She said, "I see your business is starting to struggle, I have a friend who is in the business of saving failing operations. It's not uncommon to see a decline in the first six months."

Kourtney quickly agreed to the meeting, she wanted to do what she could to keep her business open.

A few days later there was a knock on the door. Kourtney went to open the door, there stood four people, it was the lady that arranged the meeting, two built gentlemen wearing dark sunglasses and all black. Behind them stood a small frail gentleman.

He stepped from between the two men, "We are here to talk about saving this building."

With some hesitation, she let them in, directed them to her office, and offered them something to drink.

"Yes," the frail man said, "we would like two coffees and two waters please." When she returned everyone was seated at the conference table. "Let's cut to the chase, your business is struggling, you want to keep it open, and I am here to help."

"What kind of help would you provide my business?" She asked.

"Here's my business suggestions, take a few minutes too look it over while we enjoy this lovely hospitality." Kourtney stopped a few times at things she wasn't sure of or just didn't like. Kourtney put down the paperwork and began to drink her coffee.

"What do you think?"

"Well," she replied. "My club runs from 7:00 pm until midnight, with no alcohol. This says you want the club to run from 7:00 pm until 3:00 am, more dancers and you want to serve alcohol." She stood up, "No! This is not what I want to do, this is not my vision." When she stood up the large men stood up also, walking behind her placing their hands on her shoulder in a gesture to sit back down.

"We are not asking you to agree, your business is failing, and this is what we are going to do to save it. For the use of this nightclub with all of our requests you will get a 25,000-dollar deposit, then for the next several weeks you will get paid $10,000 a week to run your business. You will get to run your business for five days and we get it for that one night.

"You will be our hostess, there will be a back of the house set up, that you will not have access to or need to go back there. Our VIP's will pay $5,000 a person, everything is top shelf back there. From those sales you will get an additional 10% added to your weekly payment."

She looked puzzled, "How can you make that much money in one night?"

"Again, that is not your concern."

"When will this begin?"

He responded with a loud, firm voice "NOW! We are looking at a three-month deal."

Kourtney was not happy with it, but what choice did she have? With each weekend that passed, she saw the amount of money that was coming in, she started to become greedy, so greedy that Kourtney asked if they wanted to stay later or if they wanted to use Friday night as well. If they stayed longer on Saturdays, her amount per week would go from $10,000 to $18,500. Her backroom percentage would go from 10% to 12%.

All Kourtney could see now was the money. As the crowds increased, so did her need for security. Kourtney hired a new bouncer and a new dancer for the back room. When the interviews were over, she walked the men to the door, there stood the preacher. She thanked the gentlemen for their time an invited in the preacher.

"I will get to the point of my visit," he said. "Over the last few months, the community center has taken on a new look, do you care to explain?"

"I now have a business partner who came in to save my business because it was beginning to fail. At the pace the center was going I would be in foreclosure. Mr. Smalls is keeping me out of foreclosure, and I can pay my weekly employees.

"I have done everything to keep the community center side of things separate from the club side. Take a walk with me I want to show you something."

She took him down the hall to see the section of the center that was dedicated to the church. "I promised the board that I would respect and honor all that you all have done for me. And I plan to do just that. It is Saturday nights only, I have the club heavily secured, to protect the people inside as well as anything else that could happen. We have been doing this for a little over a month. So far, we have had no incidents."

The preacher sat back in his chair, took a deep breath. He responded, "I will give you two weeks, no more than three, to break ties with this group. If you have not closed this club side of the business down, you will turn this building over to the person listed in clause 3.4."

"What clause?" He pulled the contract out of his briefcase, pointing to the clause 3.4. and Kourtney fell back in the chair. The preacher asked her if she had not seen or read it when she signed the paperwork.

"No!" she said, "I did not."

He said that he would return in three weeks to see that this matter had been taken care of. She collapsed in her chair and began to cry.

Jon, the new bouncer, didn't leave the building. He was in the hallway listening to the conversation. Jon walked into Kourtney's office, "Are you ok?"

She replied, "I am fine, why are you still here?"

"I had questions about my pay and the hours. I forgot to ask them while I was here."

Kourtney yelled, "You couldn't send an email?" As she continued to cry, Jon handed her a box of tissues.

"Thank you," she responded, "I didn't mean to be so harsh; you work Saturdays from 6:00pm to 3:00am Sunday morning. You get a flat rate of $800.00 a night and 1% of the door collections."

"That's very generous, thank you." Jon responded. "I am sorry that I bothered you, here's my personal number if you need anything please call." She smiled and told him thank you.

As the weeks went on, Kourtney and Jon grew close, they were getting to know each other on a personal level. She was starting to trust him, she told him the entire story with the preacher. Jon told her not to worry. Jon held true to his statement. Jon set up a meeting with the preacher at the local coffee shop. Jon greeted the preacher with a handshake and thanked him for coming.

The preacher began with, "There's nothing you can say to keep me from taking that warehouse from her, to use it for the good of the community as promised."

Jon with his hands raised, "Please hear me out. I am Gondry Fitz, I am an undercover police officer working to arrest the people that are using Kourtney for a store front to launder money. We have several weeks of information on the operation, and we are just a few weeks from multiple arrest.

"Just like yourself, we want to rid the community of people like this. If you go through now with taking the business from her, we will lose this opportunity to stop them. We have been following them for years and this is the first time we got this close."

With a look of confusion, he asked how much of this Kourtney was involved with. Jon responded that she didn't know what was going on in the back rooms, they would not let her in.

"All she knows is that as long as they are in the warehouse, she gets a flat fee of $10,000 a week. Her plan was to do this for a month to get the warehouse back on its feet. Something happened and they are now staying longer."

"I have one more question," the preacher said, "is Kourtney working with you to help end this mess?"

"No Sir, she knows nothing of why my partner, and I got a job there. You are the only one that knows."

The preacher agreed to keep his secret, thanked him for shedding light on why Kourtney had been acting different for a while. "Good luck, keep me posted if you need anything from the church."

Jon stayed in the coffee shop for a while, he was thinking about his feelings for Kourtney. How would this mess with his ability to do his job? *She trusts me and I trust her, I think this weekend is the right time to tell her who I am and what is going on. What if I tell her and she tells the old man, the case is ruined, and I will lose my job. Is that a risk I am willing to take?*

Saturday came and it was time to talk to Kourtney. Jon knocked on her office door, "Hey can we talk?"

"Yes, come in."

"No, can we go outside to talk?" If they walked around outside, there would be no chances of someone hearing them or her office being bugged. Once they were outside, he began.

"I want to talk to you about something."

Kourtney nodded, "Go ahead."

"Since I have gotten to know you, the lines here have been blurred."

"What do you mean," she asked.

"I am falling in love with you," at that moment she stopped walking.

"You are what?"

"I am in love with you, and we need to talk before this goes any further."

"Okay I am listening," he reached into his pocket and pulled out his badge.

"What is this?"

"I am a undercover police officer here to stop the things that are going on at your warehouse. The man in the back is running one of the largest money laundering rings out of your warehouse. It takes about five hours to clean money, have you ever noticed that you get a liquor delivery every week but there is nothing new on the shelf? Also, you are not allowed to go to the back room since they took over the club."

Kourtney was angry because he lied to her. Jon apologized repeatedly to her.

She responded, "Give me some time."

Jon pleaded with her not to say anything, even though she was mad at him, she agreed not to say anything. She had a question for Jon. "Do I have to give their back?"

"I am not sure, I never heard anything about him paying money to you," he said with a wink." Let's keep it that way, from this point on any money that he pays you, do not deposit it in the bank. Keep it in a lock box out of sight."

She understood what she needed to do. "Wait, there's something else," she said. "For a month or so, when I am finished with my exercise class it feels like someone is following me. Or they are lurking in the parking lot. Do you think its them?"

Jon looked around, "I am not sure if it's them or not, but we need to be extremely careful about when and where we talk. How we are seen together and no kissing in public. We hadn't kissed yet," Jon leaned over and kissed her. "Now we have," he said.

Blushing, she agrees to the terms, Jon agreed that he would be in the parking lot when she leaves. Nothing would happen to her while he was around. Hearing that made Kourtney relax a bit. Jon apologized to her again for lying to her. She nodded, with acceptance of his apology.

"Let's get back inside before someone notices that we are both gone. To help you feel more at ease there are four undercover police officers working in your warehouse. I can't tell you who they are but trust me you are well protected."

Jon's phone rang, "Hey we got information that they are moving locations at the end of the night with plans to burn the warehouse to the ground. They don't want any evidence that they had been there."

"So, what's the plan?" Jon asked.

"Let the first truck come in as usual, when the second truck pulls up, we will come in with a SWAT team alongside of it to break into the warehouse. We need crowd control tonight. The less people inside the less chance we will have of injuries or deaths. Only let a few people in tonight, make an excuse because you can't let people in like the previous night. Those that you turn away let them know that they will all get V.I.P. passes for another night to make up for not getting in.

"If we must use our guns, we won't have to worry about a stampede of any kind. You will get a text when it is time to move people out. When you get that text message you will have five minutes to put people in place and clear the warehouse. Keep

Kourtney at the front door as the hostess, that way she can get out of the building easily."

"Okay, we are all set on this end," Jon replied, then he turned to Kourtney to inform her of what was going to happen.

She was scared about what was going to happen, but Jon promised that he would hold up her end of the deal no matter how scared she was. It was time to open the club, Kourtney was working the front door greeting customers as planned. The old man came into the club, walked past her without saying anything. There were fifty ladies in the club, now she had to begin turning the ladies away. With V.I.P. invites in hand, she turned them away. Telling them that the water pipe had burst, and they were working on clearing out the club as they spoke.

Her phone buzzed, it was Jon.

"We have eight minutes to clear the club. I will ring your phone when you have two minutes to get out of here. I need you to get in your car and drive until you hear from me again."

She let the people outside know that she thinks they have hit a gas line and she wanted everyone to please leave quickly. The guests start to run to their cars. Then inside, she makes an announcement over the DJ's mike, that a possible gas leak had been reported. "Please clear immediately. You can get your V.I.P. pass as you go out the door. Please HURRY!" she instructs in a calm yet firm voice.

The ladies did as instructed, fifty ladies were cleared from the club and the parking lot without any issues. Jon saw that the dancers hadn't left the building yet. She ran into the dressing room, "There's a gas leak grab your shit and let's go!"

"What about our payment for tonight?" She dropped five thousand dollars in front of them all. "Here's your money for tonight plus a tip. Now, GO!"

As the dancers were running for the door, some dressed and others with just their shorts on, there was a loud boom coming from the back. She screamed again "GO, RUN, GET OUT OF HERE!"

They all ran out the front door to the parking lot. She noticed that three of the dancers didn't come out. Those must be the undercover dancers/police. Another loud boom came from the building, the police were now in the front, the back, the sides, she believed that they were on the roof of the warehouse as well.

People in handcuffs started to come out of the building, one-by-one they yelled at Kourtney that she had set them up. She became upset yet stayed calm as the comments and threats started to come her way. It felt like the temperature had dropped twenty degrees when the old man stopped in front of her. With a stern voice filled with hatred "You did this to me. My family has lost everything, don't go to sleep, watch your back until the day you die."

With those words, Kourtney felt a fear she had never felt before. That night she stayed at Jon's house for safety reasons. The next morning, he suggested she stay with him for a few weeks or at least until they knew the old man would not make bail. At first, she didn't agree but then she changed her mind. This could be a good time to get to know more about him. Jon took Kourtney to her apartment, so she could get all the things she would need for a few weeks.

She unlocked the door, and her apartment was trashed with a message painted on the wall, "Watch your back bitch!" Kourtney fell to the floor in tears. Jon called for back-up to her apartment, he told her that she couldn't go in. Her apartment was now a crime scene. Backup arrived and they entered the apartment, with Kourtney safe in the hallway with another officer. As they walked through the apartment, there were photos of Jon and Kourtney in the parking lot together, photos of them kissing thrown over the floor.

The police asked Jon to leave he would meet him outside in a few minutes. Twenty minutes later, he came out of the apartment to talk to them both. "We can't allow you to return home. I have called for a squad car to take you both to an unknown location. Once we know the outcome of this, you can return home. Jon, can I talk to you for a minute?" Jon walked over, "How long has this been going on?"

"I have been attracted to her from the moment I stepped into the building, yesterday was the first time I acted on my feelings."

The officer looked at him for a few minutes, he believed him. "Jon, I will back you on this because you have never lied to me in the past."

Kourtney and Jon arrived at a beautiful mountain cabin, it was stocked with food and clothes for them both. Jon phone beeped, the message read, "It looks like you two will be there for three or four days."

The old man would not go before the judge for two days, once the police know what would happen to him then they could be better prepared, to return Kourtney and Jon home. Over the next few days, the two got to know each other. They talked about hopes, dreams, and where they saw themselves in five years. They took long walks in the woods. Kourtney had not been this relaxed in a while.

Jon got a message that there was a car coming to pick them up. "We had a cleaning crew take care of Kourtney's apartment. Both of you will have bodyguards, until the trial is completed."

She was excited to return to her apartment. Once there, it was like nothing ever happened. She began to work on her social media to launch a re-opening for next week. All next week the classes would be free, and the church would be there every other Sunday for church services for the community.

The preacher saw her the post, before she could reach out to him. He sent a message, "Glad you are safe, and this mess is behind you."

She replied, "Thank you for not giving up on me and the vision for the warehouse. I promise if I find myself needing help again, I will reach out to you and the church."

He was happy to see that. As she finished her message to the preacher, her phone buzzed, it was Jon, "Rose are red, violets are blue, I like you and you like me too. Wanna be my girlfriend?" she couldn't help but to laugh out loud and responded quickly, "YES!"

Now that they were officially dating and no longer had to hide it, she returned to teaching classes. That feeling that she had before returned. She began to look over her shoulder, feeling uneasy, she told her bodyguard about her feelings. She also told Jon; he said he would meet her after her classes to walk her to the car.

With Jon and the bodyguard walking her to her car at night, her fears started to ease. On Monday, she had booked a double class and Jon was unable to be there when she finished. She told him not to worry about it because the bodyguard was there, and she was okay. Reggie, her bodyguard, was ready to walk to the car, he stopped, and she asked what was wrong, "Are you ok?"

He said, "Yes, I forgot my briefcase. Let's go back in."

Kourtney said, "No, you go in I will be okay."

"Stay right here," Reggie said.

"Don't worry, I will be fine, go get your bag. I will stand here under the light until you get back."

While Reggie was inside, she began to put her stuff in the car, when she heard footsteps. She said, "That didn't take you long, I told you I would be okay." She turned to see that it wasn't Reggie standing there.

"Hey what are you doing here? How did you know how to find me? You need, to leave now! My bodyguard is inside, you don't want him to come out here and see you. Stop walking towards me, I will scream! Stop get back."

Reggie came outside, "Kourtney, did you get tired of waiting for me? Where are you?" He walked to the other side of the car, there was a small toy SUV on fire and no Kourtney. He called 911 to report what happened. Then he called Jon to tell him he needed to rush to the warehouse.

POLICE SUMMARY REPORT

"Thank you for calling the 527 precinct, how can we help you?"

"Hey, Charlie, this is Reggie, can you send out officers to the Bridges community center?"

"What's going on man? Are you serious? Okay I will dispatch now."

The operator turned in his seat, "Hey Bates and Hill, the case you are working on, did it have a burning toy SUV?"

Bates responded, "Yes it did, why do you ask?"

"Reggie, who was assigned to the lady that owns the community warehouse is now gone, and there's a burning SUV at the location of her car."

Bates and Hill grabbed their coats and ran out the door. When they arrived at the location, next to Kourtney's car was a charred toy SUV. Like the one at Reya's house. The first question they asked, "Do the security cameras work?"

Reggie responded, "Yes, all the cameras are working."

"I need you to pull the footage, now why was it that you were not with her when she disappeared?" At that point, Reggie dropped his head.

Reggie responded, "I left my brief case in the warehouse, I asked her to come back inside with me. She insisted that I go back inside she would be okay for a few minutes, and that was exactly the amount of time that I was gone. Ten minutes at the most." As Reggie was finishing his story, Hill started yelling at Reggie, "We don't care if you had to take a piss, you were supposed to take her with you no matter where you went. She was our prime witness."

While Hill was raking Reggie over the coals, Jon pulled up. Jon wasn't out of the car before he started yelling, "Where is she?

Where's Kourtney?" Jon ran straight to Reggie, grabbed him by the shirt and began shaking him and yelling at the same time.

"Ok, everyone calm down! Reggie is taking us inside to look at the footage from the cameras. Let's work together on getting answers and find her. We will worry about punishment later if they are warranted." Everyone headed into the warehouse, Reggie said, "Kourtney has a small room that she made look like an equipment room to hide the surveillance equipment."

They all took a seat, began to go over the footage. Going back two hours, so they could see what cars were in the parking lot. This showed when the parking lot was full. Slowly the cars started to leave until there were only three cars left in the parking lot. One was Reggie's, Kourtney's and one they hadn't seen before.

As they continued to watch the footage, into the frame walked Kourtney and Reggie. You can see from Reggie's actions he was trying to get her to return to the warehouse with him, she was refusing. Reggie threw his hands up in frustration, turned and ran back into the building.

She began to load her car, and into the footage someone walked towards her. The person's back was turned to the camera, as Kourtney was turning to talk to the person, something that looked like a flash of lighting came across the screen, the camera was blurred for a few minutes. Once the focus became clear again, there was nothing left but the burning SUV, her shoes slowly going out to the camera's view as if she was being dragged away.

Jon stood up slapping the table, "What the Hell just happened? Oh, My Goodness she is gone. What do we do now?" Everyone was looking at each other.

Bates stood up, "Give me that footage Reggie, let's go back to the office."

3

LYSSA

Lyssa stood in shock, she looked at Harper, "What are we going to do now?"

Harper replied, "We must do the best we can and move on with life."

Lyssa said, "This is going to be hard, but I have no other choice I will push through."

With each day Lyssa began to get stronger. Strong enough to start with her training classes. The first time returning to the gym was hard for her. This is where she and Justice met, talking to herself *you got this, take one day at a time.*

IT was Tuesday, this day was no different from the others. She set up her class for the intermediate body workout, she got a text that her class would be full. A C.E.O of an online business booked her class for a team building exercise. There was enough space to host the 18 people that would be in attendance. For short notice, she was given a $1,000 bonus in addition to her usual fee.

On time, the group walked in and they were excited to be there. Two of the men were having a conversation about how beautiful she was. Lyssa began to blush after hearing the conversation.

"Hello everyone, let's begin." While teaching the class you could hear people, saying "ouch, oh lord make it stop, how much longer is this class?" But not the two men, they were trying to outdo each other to get her attention.

Once class was over, both men walked over to her. They handed her their business cards, pushing each other's hand away like two little kids. She took both cards then gave them hers. I look forward to seeing you in my upcoming classes. For a while both men attended her class. Mason stop attending after four classes in, because Lyssa told him that she was not going out with him.

Tucker continued taking her class. During breaks in the class, they got to know each other. To their surprise, they had similar goals. They both were driven; she wanted to run her own business. He wanted to have multiple businesses around the world. Tucker had become a permanent fixture in her class, after her classes were complete, they would go for a run then stop at the smoothie café.

He told her how beautiful she was, she told him that he made her feel safe and valued. Lyssa continued to talk about owning multiple exercise spas. Tucker asked if she had a business proposal written up.

Lyssa replied, "I have one. No one ever took me seriously."

"Would you be able to bring it with you to the next class? I may have someone who would be willing to take a chance on your vision."

With excitement in her voice, Lyssa agreed to bring the papers with her. It was time to go home, the store was closing. They exchanged a hug, "Text me when you are home safely."

"I will!" she replied. Lyssa arrived at her apartment building, but she had a strange feeling when a cold chill came over her. As she continued to walk to her apartment, she thought she heard footsteps behind her. When she turned there was no one there.

Once inside her apartment, she grabbed a water bottle and flopped down on the sofa. She texted Tucker to let him know she was at home, this text started hours of messages between the two. The sun was coming up, "Oh no, I have to be in the gym earlier today, this is going to be a long day."

Tucker responded, "I wish all my days would start and end with you."

She dropped the phone with a gasp. "What are you saying she replied?"

"I would like for this to progress into a relationship. Is that something you would be interested in?" Without hesitation, she said yes to Tucker.

He continued, "I would like to make this official, Lyssa would you like to go on a date with me this Friday?" She giggled like a high school girl.

"Yes, I would love to go out with you. Where should I meet you?"

"That's not needed, send me your address and I will handle the rest. Also remember to bring the proposal with you. I look forward to seeing you on Friday." As soon as the messaging ended, Lyssa cancelled all of her classes for the day. She asked the owners not to open her side of the gym that day.

Lyssa called Harper, she wanted to know if she could come over ASAP? She told her she could get there in less than an hour. Lyssa told her of the conversation. Harper was happy for her "Let's go to lunch, shopping, and then dinner. Friday will get here fast, and you need to look amazing."

Harper was correct, Friday was now there. Her phone buzzed, "Please head downstairs." As Lyssa reached the ground floor, there stood Tucker, he opened the door for her, in her seat was a beautiful arrangement of flowers and a gift. Tucker asked her to not open it until the date was over. Everything was perfect, she handed her proposal over to him. It covered in detail how she would like to have multiple centers around the city.

He asked many questions, "What was the number of centers she wanted? How would she oversee them all? Where did she see herself in five years?" Lyssa was starting to get pissed, because of all the questions he was asking.

What business was it of his, you just need to take my paperwork to your friend, she said to herself. She was about to snatch back her papers when Tucker began to speak.

"Everything looks in order, have you found where your first center will be located?"

"Yes, I would like to purchase the one that I am currently in."

"Excellent," he said, "I have seen the for sale sign out front. Do you know what the asking price is?"

"Yes, I do, they are asking for $782,500.00. Why?"

Tucker reached into his jacket, pulled out a small folder, he began to write. Lyssa couldn't see what he was doing, then you could hear paper tears. He handed her a check for $780,000.00. "Offer this to the owner if he turns you down over twenty-five hundred dollars. He doesn't want to sell the building."

"What are you doing? Who are you? How can you have money like that, and you just hand it over?"

"I am the CEO of an online dating service. I specialize in connecting people after a thorough interview process. My company has an 87.2% success rate. Yes, I am single because I havn't found that special someone until now."

"Who me?" She asked.

"Yes, you. After I took your class, I couldn't get you off my mind. You are smart, funny, and everything that I am looking for in a partnership."

"Thank you," she responded. "I am attracted to you and would like to learn more about you." Tucker responded, "Let's go for walk."

They took a stroll around one of the lakes in the city. They talked until midnight. Once they arrived back to the car, he told her that she could open the box. In the box was a key, "what is this for?" Lyssa asked.

"Clear your schedule tomorrow, and the key will make sense. When I get home, I will take care of clearing my schedule. Here's the address that I need you to meet me at."

After clearing her schedule, she picked out clothes to wear for the next, she was very nervous, and unable to sleep. After flipping and flopping the sun was finally up, and it was time to get ready. When they arrived at the location, there were over 100 people walking around. There were photos of Lyssa all over the place. She called Harper, can you get here fast? I don't know what is happening here.

She walked around confused and looking for Tucker. Once he was located, he was so excited to see her. He extended his hand, "Hello I am Tucker, I hear nothing but good things about you. I am glad you are here." Lyssa was confused but played along. "Do you still have the key that I gave you?"

"I do," she replied.

"Good walk with me, get the key out, we are about to have fun."

Tucker and Lyssa walked up the stairs, toward a podium that was in front of a beautiful building. Tucker began to welcome everyone that was in attendance. "We are here today for a very special lady. I met her in a team-building class a few months ago. Since that class she has stolen my heart." Lyssa looked out into the crowd; she located family and friends standing alongside of her mother. She then found Harper standing in the back of the crowd, with a smile and nod of support.

Tucker continued, "During that time, I learned about her vison, hopes, dreams, and desires. This center is one of them, please join me as I give this center to her and the community." He handed her scissors and asked her to please cut the ribbon. The center opened. As the crowd came in, Tucker said, "I have another surprise for you." He asked her to enter one of the workout rooms, he turned to the crowd and asked them to stay quiet.

The room was filled with white roses, music was playing and champagne glasses everywhere. Her smile was big as she turned back to him and he was on bended knee, "Lyssa, I know it's been a short time, I know you are the one for me. Would you please do me the honor of marrying me?"

She immediately said, "Yes!" The crowd erupted into cheers. "I have one more question for you. Do you have any plans for the next ten days?"

"I am in the middle of classes, why?"

"We leave in two days to head to Dubia to get married." Again, the crowd cheered, she searched the room for Harper, there she stood with her mother both giving the sign of approval. As the guests were coming in some had gotten a golden envelope. Holding Lyssa's hand, he asked the crowd, "If you got a golden envelope, please hold it up."

Over fifty people held up a golden envelope. Tucker asked them to open it. There were tears, cheers, and one woman fainted. Those who got the envelope received an all-expense paid trip to Dubia to attend the wedding. The party continued as they celebrated the engagement, wedding, and the new building.

The next day Lyssa took the check to the owner of her building. Once they verified that the money was there, the building was hers. The paperwork will be ready in 20 days.

"No problem." She responded. *Now to find Harper and get a wedding dress.* She only had two and a half days before they left.

As she was sending a message to Harper, Tucker sent a text message "You have an appointment at 1:00 today to get your dress. Harper will be there along with other family members and friends."

When she arrived to the shop the entire store was closed down. Tucker had the shop closed for her to get the attention she needed to get the perfect dress and the bridesmaids' dresses needed for the wedding. The owner told Lyssa and her group to pick whatever they wanted; the bill has been handled.

She started to cry. The store owner told her to stop, "Let's have fun picking out your dress." Lyssa tried to drink the champagne, but she didn't feel well at all, but pushed through to find her dream dress. She got a beautiful lace, floor length, off-the-shoulder wedding dress. Her second was a knee length beach style lace dress. The ladies in the group were able to pick the dress that they like in beautiful beach colors.

This was so much fun. Lyssa is planning a dream wedding without any stress. She just wished she was feeling better. All she needed to get was the dress.

She packed her suitcase and headed to the airport. She arrived an hour early. In the lobby were over 100 people waiting to leave. Tucker grabbed the microphone, "Hello everyone, there are two check-in stations to board the plane. If you are related to the bride or groom, please board on the left side, and our guest please board on the right side."

Tucker had a private plane for the wedding party and close family. When they boarded the plane, there was food, drinks, movies, music and a private chef. Before the plane landed with the guest and family, they all got envelopes and Welcome/Thank you boxes. On the private plane the chef prepared meals and they shared stories and exchanged laughter.

Tucker opened the closet, and he began to pull out additional boxes made just for the weeding party. His assistant came over to help, but he told her to sit back and relax he had it. Inside the boxes were watches and bracelets from Tiffany's, a photo album and handwritten note of thanks for joining them on this adventure. As the plane was landing, Lyssa was not feeling well, the gift for her would have to wait. There was a meet and greet later that night, but she was unable to attend the event. Harper stayed behind her so that Tucker could address the group and continue with the party.

There was a knock on the door, the hotel doctor came to see what he was wrong and how could help her. He took a few samples; one was a blood sample, and the other was to check for the flu. He returned to his office to get the results. Two hours later, the doctor returned to give her the results. He took a deep breath, looked down at his paperwork. "You need to keep crackers and ginger ale with you at all times."

When you return home, you will need to take one room and turn it into a nursey. Lyssa fell back on the bed, she looked at Harper, "Please don't say anything."

Harper was in shock, how did this happen, "You never said that you two did it."

"I was trying to tell you everything, but yes, we have evidently did it. UGH! What am I going to do now?"

"You need to go to sleep and get as much rest as you can before tomorrow."

It was morning, Lyssa woke up to pounding on her door. It was the wedding crew ready to do hair and make-up. Lyssa was getting ready behind double doors, so no one could see her until she was finished. When the doors opened, the bridal party started to cry. Everyone was called to the beach; the backdrop was like a photo. Crystal clear waters and beautiful white sands with a gentle breeze.

As Lyssa began to walk down the aisle, she began to get dizzy, she paused for a second. Not to draw attention to how she was feeling she waved to the guest and smiled. Tucker and Lyssa are exchanging their vows when the official asked if anyone had a reason for them to not get married to speak up.

At that moment, Lyssa passed out. The guest started to run to her, as she began to open her eyes, the doctor was standing over her. She looked at everyone, "Please I am okay, can you bring me a chair? I would like to get married." with a chuckle. When she laughed everyone else began to laugh.

Tucker asked for a chair, he wanted to sit down so that they could be on the same level. Once they were married, Tucker picked her up and carried her down the aisle. He was going to take her back to the room, she insisted that she wanted to enjoy the reception. She promised that if she didn't feel well, she would let her husband know. Tucker could do nothing but smile at her, calling him her husband.

During the reception, he made a beautiful speech, he thanked all that joined them to make this beautiful day. Lyssa asked for the mic, she looked at Tucker, "You have made this the wedding of my dreams, you have been the piece in my life that was missing. I feel that our future will be bright, and our home will be full of love, happiness, and little feet."

She handed Tucker a box, "This is my wedding gift to you." Inside the box was a t-shirt that read "Dad's #1 fan." Tucker jumped for joy because he was so happy to hear that he would be a father. Tucker handed her a box, in it was a remote.

She asked, "What is this for?"

"Point it toward the screen." Tucker appeared on the screen, "Thank you for marrying me, I am the happiest person in the world to have you in my life. When we return home, this is where you are going to live."

He took a step to the side, behind him was a lovely six-bedroom, four-bathroom house with a pool, and assistants to help with home maintenance. Everyone was excited, she turned to him gave him a hug, she said, "I can't wait to get home and be your wife."

The reception went into the wee hours of the morning. Lyssa sipped ginger ale, and nibbed on bread that helped her get through the night.

At lunchtime the next day there was two busses waiting in front of the hotel to take a tour of the island before they return home in two days. Lyssa stayed behind to take care of herself. She was in a rush to return home so she began to pack the suitcases. There was a knock on the door, her wedding photo arrived before they left the island. The buses started to return, Tucker returns to the room, as he was getting settled in, the concierge knocked on the door with some disturbing news.

There was a storm heading their way and it was expected to hit land late the next day. He had taken the liberty to have the planes at the airport in the next two hours. "We are contacting your entire party, to have them pack and meet us downstairs in two hours. There is no need to panic this is safety for our guests. I will check back in with you guys in an hour to see if you need any additional assistance."

No one went into panic mode. Everyone was okay with the early departure. Tucker made a few phone calls to set up some entertainment and things for the passengers to ease the trip back home. Everyone made it to the airport; they all were still in party mode which made Tucker and Lyssa happy that no one was upset to leave early.

Everyone boarded the plane singing, laughing, and with joy everywhere. When they got to their seats, they had blankets, head rest, and their own package of wedding photos. How did he get this done so fast? He had his assistant and the concierge work together to get everything needed. Safely home and married Lyssa begins to plan how she was going to run two businesses and be pregnant at the same time.

As she began to work on the plan, Tucker came in with a young lady, "Hey Lyssa, I would like to introduce you to your personal assistant Jessie." Lyssa was excited to have the help and trusted Tucker's judgement on the business side.

She had a lunch date with Harper to see how she had been since the wedding. Walking into the restaurant, she has a weird feeling that someone was behind her, she turned around but there was no one there. *I must be going crazy.*

Harper and Lyssa had a good lunch, talking about the wedding, the baby, and the new house. Harper wanted to know how she was going to take care of both buildings and have the baby?

"Tucker got me a personal assistant named Jessie. So, my load is not as heavy as I thought it would be. I would like to have a grand opening before I have the baby. Can you help me oversee that they get done?"

"Yes, I can do that with the help of your assistant we will get this done. Have you gone to the doctor to get a due date?"

"The baby is due in five to six months from now. We have plenty of time to get this done. Tucker has the floorplan so that is not a problem."

"When I get the floorplans let's meet so that you can tell me what's supposed to be in the rooms and what colors you see for the buildings. Are you ok?" Harper asked.

"No, I am not, I feel like someone is following me. When I turn around there's no one there. I am trying to no freak out; it could all just be me being pregnant and my body is out of whack."

"What are your plans for your classes? I have cut my classes to one or two a week when I am home, I am working on the gala for the grand openings for the building. I could just be exhausted with my minds playing tricks on me." Tucker stopped by to drop off the floorplan before lunch was over.

When Lyssa went to the restroom; Tucker turned to Harper and said, "This is a perfect time to talk to you."

"What's up? Harper asked.

"I know that she has you designing the buildings, do you think you can squeeze in a baby shower also?"

"It would be my pleasure to get this together for you."

He handed her two credit cards," This one it to purchase everything needed to get the buildings the way she wants them, spare no expense. The second one is for the baby shower, also spare no expense for this event. I would like it to take place at the house. I am not sure how we are going to pull this off, but I know we will get it done."

As Harper and Tucker were setting the date for the shower, Lyssa returned, she wanted to go home as she was not feeling well.

"Tucker, can you call the doctor and ask him to come to the house, please? Nothing to worry about, I just want a checkup and I don't want to go to the hospital. Harper can you take me home, please?"

"I will be happy to take you home," she said.

The doctor was at this house before they got home waiting for her.

He checked her out, Harper entered the room, "Is everything okay?"

"Yes, we are all fine," the doctor said.

"We will need to put her on limited work and bedrest, but other than that she is fine. The next few months will go by quickly."

She called Tucker to let him know. He suggested that she work on paperwork and stuff on the laptop and let others do the leg work.

Over the next few months, Harper and Jessie worked on the buildings to get them done the way Lyssa wanted them. The plans for the baby shower were also coming together. Lyssa was able to plan a very elegant gala for the ribbon cutting ceremony. She was also approved by her doctor to attend the ceremony if she was seated 90% of the time.

As Lyssa lied in her bed, she could see the beautiful view of her estate. In walked Tucker, "I got the okay from the doctor to take you for ride." She was more than excited to leave the bed and the house.

As the two took off for their drive, Harper sent a text message "All clear." Ten minutes later, three vans pulled up and ten people jumped out. Within three hours, the crew was able to turn the backyard into a lavish baby shower. The colors were all neutral, but bright and vibrant, the next thing was to get the guest there. She was running out of time.

Three miles down the street was a church. Harper made a large donation to use the parking lot. She sent another text message, "Ready." The guest began to load the bus, once at the house, she told everyone to relax they were twenty minutes away. Lyssa returned home. She was tired, and her feet were swollen. She was heading upstairs, when Harper said, "Let's relax by the pool for a little bit then you can go upstairs."

She agreed, as she opened the doors, there stood over a hundred guests. Tears began to flow down her face. "I am so grateful to you all." She sat down and put her feet up. The guest brought the gifts to her, so she could stay seated. As they finished the last gift, she stood up with Tucker by her side, "I would like to thank everyone that came to support our blessing. To see you here today means more to me than you will ever know."

In the crowd you could see the wait staff handing the guest envelopes. While this was taking place, Tucker then took the mic, and asked Lyssa to take a seat. "I too would thank everyone for coming, in a few weeks we are having a grand opening gala, you are all invited. Thank you for being a part of our lives. We look forward to seeing you at the event as we continue to celebrate my wife and her accomplishments."

With four months left to go, Harper began to take complete charge of everything in the final stages for the gala. As they got closer to the date, she noticed that things were happening as she worked on the event. It started with the event permit getting denied. She called a friend in the office to help with getting the permit issued. Next the caterer cancelled, his reason was he wouldn't have the staff to cover the size of the crowd. This time Harper called friends and family who would be willing to work at the event due to the staffing issues. They agreed with help in place the caterer agreed to continue with the meal plan.

The issues continued. The live band that she had arranged was double booked, so they cancelled the gala based on who would pay the most for them to play. The band member suggested a DJ - the crowd would love it and could make requests. Harper couldn't believe this was happening. It seemed odd but she didn't have time to investigate it.

The day of the event had arrived, Tucker stopped by the cleaners to get Lyssa's dress. The cleaners had lost the dress for the gala, it was a custom-made dress, due to her being so close to her due date, and she had gained a lot of weight. Harper sent Jessie to a local boutique with a photo of the dress that was lost. She asked her to get anything close to the dress and make sure it was fabulous.

Harper had again, put out another fire. She got a call that the van with the table and chairs had broken down fifteen minutes from the event. Harper was wondering how much more could happen without her having to tell Lyssa that this event it trying to fall apart all around them. A tow truck was sent out to get the truck to the event.

Lyssa was in the dressing room nervous for another reason. She was keeping a secret from everyone that she was going to share that night. As she sat waiting for her dress to show up, Harper and Tucker somehow managed to get the ballroom set up. Jessie arrived in a beautiful dress. Now it was time to share with Lyssa all the drama that had gone on in the last few weeks that they kept from her. Everything was taken care of so there was no need for her to be upset, the dress Jessie got her fit perfectly, she looked like a princess.

As the event started, the host and hostess were giving interviews to the local news outlets. Dinner was being served; everyone was having a good time. Then everyone heard a tapping on the glass and the room became quiet. The host and hostess started to say thank you to everyone that came out to support them. "In the coming weeks the classes offered will be online, and we both hope that you will attend at either location." He hands the mic to Lyssa, she agreed with the message that he had said.

Today had turned out great even with all the setbacks. "I would like to thank my good friend Harper and my assistant Jessie along with my husband. They managed to get this event together without anyone knowing that it was falling apart behind the scenes.

"To my husband, this has been the best ten months of my life. To show you how much I appreciate you, I would like you to open one more box. Can you bring out the box please." The crowd was guessing, laughing and one person yelled "You know what happened the last time you opened a box?" The room burst into laughter as the box was handed to Tucker. The room was quiet as he took the lid off the box. He dropped the box and looked at Lyssa, Is this real? Are you kidding me?" The crowd was yelling to tell them what was in the box.

He yelled into the mic; "We are having twins!" The room erupted in cheers. "Let's start partying everyone." Lyssa and

Harper were having a great time dancing, Harper stopped, and she looked at Tucker as both of their feet were wet. Her water broke on the dance floor. She was rushed to the hospital, with half of the guests right behind them. Everyone was in the waiting room trying to figure out what they would have. What seemed like forever, Tucker comes out to let the room know that they had a boy and a girl.

"The boy is named after me, and the girl is named after Harper." There was not a dry eye in the room. Harper stayed with Lyssa for the first few weeks so that she could get used to being a mom of two. You never know how fast time goes when you are at home taking care of babies. Tucker came home, without any greetings, she turned to him. I am ready to go back to work.

He was not on board with this idea, but he knew she had to be hands-on with her buildings to make sure that they were successful. "I don't have a problem with that, as long as we have a nanny in place and support for you and the babies." She wrapped her arms around him with excitement. "Let's look at a few agencies to see who has the best of the best for our family," he responded.

While he looked for the nanny, she began to update her website with classes that would start in three weeks. She was teaching post-pregnancy classes, she could relate to this one, the moms could bring the babies with them. That class sold out for the entire month it was available.

One week into teaching classes that strange feeling returned. *I know that I am not crazy* she thought, *I hear footsteps.* It really bothered her this time so she decided that she was going to tell Tucker, maybe he could hire someone to be there late nights.

There was an emergency at the office, Tucker was late coming home, and she didn't get to talk to him.

"Classes today were great ladies, I wanted to share that we are going to offer more classes starting next week. We have a male instructor joining our team as well. We are going to have security starting next week also for the late-night classes. We want you all to feel safe while you are on the property." She thanked them all, as they left the building. It was now 9:00 pm and time to go home. On her late nights she didn't have to worry about the twins because her mother was there.

As she was walking to her car, her phone rang, and it was her mother. "Hey, I was checking to make sure that you are, okay? You are usually home by now; the twins need to be fed and I can't do that if you know what I mean." They both laughed,

"Yes, I am heading home. I am walking to the car now." Her mom asked if there were lights in the parking lot, she assured her that she was okay. The building was in a safe neighborhood." I will see you in less than an hour."

She hung up the phone with her mom, but as she is getting into the car there was a tap on her shoulder, she turned with the pepper spray in her hands ready to spray. As she turned, the pepper spray and cell phone hit the ground. She yelled, "OMG it's you. what are you doing here?"

It was now 11:00 pm Tucker had come home, but still no Lyssa. The tracker on the phone said she was still at work. They both tried calling her with no answer. They couldn't wait any longer, they put the twins in the minivan and headed to the fitness center.

When they arrived at the fitness club, her car was there. The car door was open, cell phone on the ground with the mase. As they walked around the car there was a toy SUV burning.

"Call 911, Now!" he yelled.

POLICE SUMMARY REPORT

At the station, the dispatcher yelled, "Hill, Bates you got another one. There is a toy burning at the new fitness center that just opened."

Hill yelled back to stop playing around, that this was a serious issue here.

"I am not playing here's the location." Bates looked at Hill, "What the hell is going on here?"

Four police cars along with Hill and Bates pulled into the parking lot. Bates got out the car, yelling "Don't touch anything. Who found the car?" Tucker and Lyssa's mom yelled, "We did!"

"Good evening, sir, I am officer Bates this is my partner Hill. Can you tell us why you are here and what you found?

Tucker was short and to the point: "First, this is my wife's business. Second, she told her mother she was heading home in twenty minutes – but that was 9 pm. Third, at 11 pm, she was still not home as she had stated. And fourth, I used the tracking app to see where she was It showed she was still here, so we got here, and we found this."

"Thank you for that sir, I know this is difficult and we want to help you get answers and find your wife. Do you know if your wife has cameras that cover the lot?" Tucker dropped his head; they were coming to install them the next day.

"Please don't worry, sir. There are other ways to locate your wife. Can we go inside?" Once inside, "Can you give us the list of your wife's employees and the schedule for today?" Just as Bates was going to ask another question, an officer yelled from the parking lot, "Bates get out here."

From the bushes, someone yelled, "Keep it down over there I am trying to sleep. Take all these cars and bright lights and go somewhere else." Bates snapped his fingers at one of the officers, pointing towards the bushes. You could hear the person yelling, "Get your hand off me. You can't grab me like that," as the two walk from behind the bushes, the officer was helping a homeless man in Bates direction. "Hill get over here." Hill greets him, the man responds, "Leave me alone."

"We have a few questions, and you can return to your nap. I want to know how long you have been here tonight?" As Hill pressed record on his phone.

"I live here," the man said. "Ms. Lyssa said I could have the corner behind the bushes if I promised not to bother the customers. I agreed, she brings me two meals a day and water. For spare change I keep the parking lot picked up. I have no need to beg.

"Oh Yea, when no one is in the building, I can shower three times a week. I have the best street life ever."

"Thank you, Hill, said. Did you hear or see anything tonight with Ms. Lyssa?"

"Sure did," he responded, "I heard it all."

Tucker yelled, "What did you see?"

The man told him to calm down. "Ms. Lyssa was walking to her car on her phone. She was laughing and seemed very happy. That's when I heard her say 'OMG it's you. What are you doing here? How did you find me?' then she yelled 'stop.' That's when I was getting up to help her, when I got to my feet she was gone. The only thing I can think of must have been, the person that is always in the parking lot acting like they are working out. They had on all black with a hoodie. I didn't think anything about it. Just thought they were working out."

Both Hill and Bates looked at each other at the same time, "Black Hoodie!"

Tucker asked "What, what does that mean?"

"Well, sir, it looks like we have another SUV case. She too was in the parking lot when she was taken."

Tucker asked, "Is this a pattern? A serial issue?"

"We have enough for tonight, if you would like to come down to the precinct tomorrow, we will have a layout of what we know for you."

They started to collect evidence to take it back to the stations, once at the station Bates and Hill now had set up photos, post-it notes with all information collected so far.

Bates looked at Hill, "Do you see it?"

4
HARPER

Andi was standing at the airport gate waiting for Harper to walk through the door. Harper had taken a break after all that had happened with Justice. Harper walked through the door looking relaxed, during this time she was able to write two award winning books. Harper wrote a book on the keys to surviving a tragic loss.

Taking readers through her pain of the loss and death of Justice. The other book was called Red Flags, what to do when you see them and ignore them. Andi had landed an hour before Harper. She was staying with her while her husband was out of the country. Andi was married on a cruise a few months ago. She married a senior engineer for a major home building company with global companies.

Once home, Harper and Andi went through all her beautiful wedding photos. There were smiles, laughter and sometimes tears. It has been a long time since they laughed like that. Harper told

Andi that she wanted to date again. Andi jumped up and said, "Hell no. Not all. oh no!"

Then Harper told Andi that she had decided to become a private investigator.

Andi fell back into the chair, "Have you lost your mind? Please tell me why being an author is not enough?"

"I don't want what happened to me to happen to someone else. If I can help solve one case with missing loved ones, this is not for nothing. To be left with no answers and getting no help, I don't want others to feel that pain."

"Have you told Lyssa this plan of yours?"

"I am not sharing with her until I am accepted into the program."

There was no need to worry too many people, if this didn't work out then there was nothing to have them worked up over. "So, what do you think about me dating again?"

"Do you really want me to answer that question" she replied.

"That's a fair question," Harper said.

"I am not sure why you are wanting to date again, or why you want to train to be a P.I. all of this seems sudden and quite confusing."

"Why don't we go out to a local bar like we used to for fun." Andi agreed and the ladies got dressed up and headed out to enjoy the evening like they had at the beginning of their friendship. Since Andi was married, there would be no more picking on someone. They were just there to have fun, dance, drink, and return home in one piece.

They found an upscale cigar bar, this was a place that they could relax, feel safe and have fun. Walking in, the ladies started to turn heads. Andi began her humorous self and was walking so that her left hand could be seen. Once at their seats, drinks were delivered to the table. The ladies told the waitress that they hadn't placed an order yet. She pointed to the bar, "Compliments of those gentlemen." They looked over at the bar, he raised his grass with a nod.

Andi waved a thank you with her left hand again to make sure her wedding ring was seen. Lyssa walked in the door, Harper looks at Andi, "Did you call her?"

"Yes, I did, you have to tell her what you are planning to do."

"Hey ladies, how is everyone? It's good to see you. Andi it's always nice having you around. How long are you going to be here?

"I will be here for a couple of months."

"Where did the drinks come from?" Lyssa asked. Before the ladies could answer, a deep voice answered, I sent them over and yours it on the way. The ladies looked up, there he stood, 6'4". He was wearing a dark grey double-breasted suit. He had a smile that could light up a dark room. He introduced himself as Zane and told the ladies to be safe and have a good evening.

Andi looked at Harper, "Cut to the chase tell her what you are planning to do tomorrow."

"Oh shit!" Lyssa responded.

"It's not bad, I am going tomorrow to see what is needed to become a Private Investigator."

"What the hell for?" asked Lyssa.

Harper continues, "I don't want what happened to us happen to someone else. I want to help solve mysteries and cold cases."

"How long have you felt this way?"

Harper responded for a while, "Once the police stopped giving updates on what was going on with Justice. Nothing, we don't know if he is dead, alive nothing. They just brushed us off."

"Damn I didn't know that you felt like this," Lyssa replied. "When are you going to look into this?"

"Tomorrow morning," Harper replied.

Lyssa yelled," Are you crazy? why so soon?"

"Lower your voice, yes, tomorrow first things in the morning."

"If you have your mind made up, then I will not do anything to try to change it."

"Okay ladies let's enjoy the rest of the night. I just wanted to share what was on my mind with you both before I go tomorrow morning."

Zane returned to the table with a piece of paper, handed it to Harper, and looked at the ladies. "You all have a good night get home safely," he returned his gaze back to Harper, "I will talk to you soon."

"The next time you are heading back here, give me a call. I would love to meet you here and get to know you better". She took the paper.

"Thank you," she replied. "Yes, I will call you the next time I am heading this way. Time to go home ladies, I need get some sleep for tomorrow."

The next day Harper went into the precinct, "Ma'am how can we help you?"

"I am not a ma'am; my name is Harper St. James. I would like to apply for your Private Investigator Academy."

The officer behind the desk started to laugh. "Again, sir, you are disrespecting me. I would like to join the program, is there someone else here I can talk to that is willing to help?"

Officer Rawlings came to the desk.

"How can we help you?"

"He can't help me, but maybe you can. I would like to sign up for the PI Academy and this officer finds it funny for whatever reason. He can't pull himself together long enough to give me an answer of any kind."

"You want to join?"

"Yes, I do, I guess you are going to start laughing also."

"No, I think it's great that you want to be part of that department." Rawlings took her back to meet some of the officers that have completed the training.

"Ms. St James, can you tell me why you want to join? What motivates you to want to take this career path?" She told them of the story of how Justice was in a wreck, he was not found when they put out the blaze and the police were brushing them off. "I feel I can be that person to help others get answers that the police are not willing to give."

After hearing her answer why, she was handed paperwork to complete for admission. Rawlings told her she was in luck, today was the cut-off to join the academy. After she completed the paperwork, Harper was handed a training schedule along with the classes she will attend in this mini police bootcamp. The reason for this, so she would be in shape if she needed to run, also to be prepared to carry a weapon.

Rawlings told her to follow him, she asked, "where we are going?

"In addition to making the cut-off, you are here for the first day of class." When she entered the room, it got quiet. She looked around, she was the only female in the class. When Harper found her seat, she looked up and saw a familiar face. It was Zane from the bar the night before. He walked over "Hello, I am officer Kincade, you are?" She was quick to understand what he was saying.

"I am Harper St. James."

"Welcome to the class St. James. Okay class, in front of you, there is everything you will need to complete this course. Once you have completed this course you will have the option of three precincts to choose from. This is a 12-hour a day program. It will rotate 6 hours with me in the classroom and 6 hours in the field with a different set of drills that will help you stay aware of your surroundings and do your job better.

Someone raised their hand, "Yes you in the back."

"Umm, why is she here?" The room burst into laughter.

"What do you mean, why is she here?"

"You can't see that she's a female? This is not a place for females."

Kincade cut him off, "Until she shows that she is unable to carry her own weight. Shut Up! During this time, you will have a partner, I usually let you pull straws, this time we are not. I want you all to look to your right, that is your partner until graduation."

Harper looked at her partner and smiled. It was the jerk that said she shouldn't be there. She extended her hand to her partner, "Hi I am the female in the room, nice to meet you." The room again burst into laughter. Jenkins stood up to protest.

Kincade said, "If you can't deal with your partner, you can leave now." Jenkins sat back down. Assignments were given to the teams. "Today we are starting in the field. We are going to work on building trust with your partners. Seems like some of you can you use that class now."

Jenkins looked at Harper, told her she wouldn't make it a week. She laughed in his face. "I will last longer than you."

Once outside there was an obstacle course set up. The drill officer did a demonstration of what they needed to do. The first time through they were to run the course without knowing what their time was until everyone had completed the course. Harper was the last one to complete the course. Jenkins hit another student on the arm, "watch St. James will be the slowest of all of us."

Kincade announced, "We will call you to line up." Jenkins was the first student called and Harper was called last. Jenkins leaned out of line, pointed, and laughed at her. "I would like for you all to look to your left, that is the person that finished ahead of you. Your times will be posted tomorrow when you come to class. Again, congratulations on completing your first class."

Jenkins yelled, "Wait that female beat all of us."

"Yes!" Kincade said, "And also, she got the fastest time of the class."

"No way," Jenkins scoffed.

Harper walked to her partner, "Don't worry, partner. I won't drop you." She couldn't wait to get home to tell the girls how her day went. She knew Andi and Lyssa would be waiting to hear if she was going to join only to find out she joined and had her first class. She also couldn't wait to share what an asshole her partner was. Harper was excited that she was going to be a private investigator.

Harper walked through the door, and there they were. "Where have you been all day. Why are you dressed like that. what's in that duffle bag."

"Calm down. I went to see what I needed to do, today was the last day to join and it was also the first day of class." She grabbed a bottle of wine, "You won't believe my day."

She began to tell them about the jerk at the front desk. "He was giving me shit because I was a female. Then a nice officer came out to see how he could help me. When I told him I wanted to join the program. He asked a few questions, told me that today was the last day they are accepting people. I thought I would have at least a day to prepare for class. Nope I was in the classroom of men and one jerk. He had an issue with me being a female, then he ended up being my partner.

"Then the assistant officer came in the room. You will never, and I mean never, guess who it was." Before they could even guess, Harper yelled out, "It was Zane from the cigar bar last night!"

"No way" Andi said. Lyssa continued to sit there in shock. "We played it off like we didn't know each other. We had to do an obstacle course. I got the best time as well as breaking record. That pissed off a few of my classmates. Oh, yeah, my partner was last. If he hated me before, he really hates me now. That was my day, I would love to stay with you guys and keep talking, I have to be at the station at 5:00am.

"I look forward to hanging out with you all over the weekend and we can talk about how the rest of the week went."

The harassment continued from Jenkins. If he was getting to her, he would never know. Harper continued to break records and make people angry, while others supported her. As the week went on, Zane finally had a moment to see Harper, keeping a safe distance he said to her, "You don't have a class on Sunday, how about a picnic in the park?" She flashed a quick smile and agreed. With a small chuckle, "let me get back in here and kick some ass. I will text you the time. I will pick you up," Zane said, "and yes kick ass."

She was exhausted when she got home but wanted to talk to Andi. She was feeling uneasy the last few days. Andi asked what was wrong, Harper said, "I feel like I am being followed." Andi told her she was tired and not to pay any attention to that feeling, she just needed rest. Harper was excited to tell her about Zane and the date on Sunday, they both giggled.

"What do I wear?"

"Something cute," Andi said. "He sees you daily looking like shit."

"That's not funny, Andi."

"Get some rest we will do nothing tomorrow but watch TV and find an outfit for you to wear."

Andi and Harper had so much fun Saturday, it was like old times without the dating app.

Sunday morning rolled around, and Harper had picked out two dresses, but Andi told her they were too old looking. Andi went into her closet, "here you go."

"What is this?" Harper asked.

Andi said, "Simple yet sexy, clingy but not tight. It's a give me an "A" teacher type of dress." They both laughed and fell back on the bed.

Harper agreed to wear the dress and jumped in the shower to get ready. She had a little time before he got there. Once out of the shower, Harper laid across the bed. She heard the doorbell ring. She looked out the window and it was Zane. She yelled down to Andi to get the door. Andi ran down the hall to get the door. Zane was standing there 6'4" tall, dark, and handsome. Wearing a black running suit with a dozen roses.

"Come in, Harper is running behind schedule. She will be with you in a moment."

"Please tell her to take her time we have all afternoon."

"Oh, my goodness, you are so sweet."

"Thank you," Zane responded. Harper walked into the room; Zane dropped the flowers on the floor. He was in such awe of how beautiful she was. He quickly picked up the flowers and handed them to her, "You are so very beautiful. Shall we go and enjoy the afternoon?" Harper took the flowers and responded, "let's go!"

They took a long drive before stopping at a lovely spot atop a mountain overlooking the city. Zane walked around to open her door. "This is so nice; I never knew this place was here." While she was looking at the view of the city, Zane was setting up the picnic and she turned to see if she could help him. He reached for her hand to help her sit down on the blanket.

They sat and talked for a while. They talked about what happened in the past. What drives them to do what they do. Where did they see themselves in five years. When she told him the story of Justice, he understood. He came home about five years ago to his house after being broken into. His wife and son were gone. To this day they haven't been found. Harper was in tears, she felt so bad, his loss was tragic. Zane was sharing it with her, as she looked at him, tears fell down her face. He wiped the tears from her face. "Yes, I miss my family, but I must continue to live my life."

Harper reached out to Zane to give him a hug. At that moment, their lunch changed from casual to serious. What was supposed to be a fun and light humorous date was now a serious conversation. The two were feeling closer than they did before. The sun was starting to set, it was beautiful Harper looked at Zane, "What about class? I don't want anyone to know that we are friends outside of the classroom."

His response was 5:00am-5:00pm Monday through Friday, "I don't know who you are," with a laugh to lighten the mood. Harper in turn laughed and thanked him. He stated that he would treat her the same as the rest of the men.

"Oh, did you notice that I am a female?" They started to laugh.

"It doesn't matter because you are kicking everyone's ass in the class."

The sun has disappeared behind the mountain. It was getting late, and it was time for them to head home. "We have to be at the station at 5:00am."

Andi and Lyssa were waiting for Harper to walk through the door. "What happened? We have been waiting for you to come home to hear all about the date!"

"I have an early morning, I will give you a bit of information, the date was great. We are set to do something every Sunday. I am going to bed now."

Class started promptly at 5:00am, no exceptions and no excuses. The cadets knew that they never wanted to give an excuse; it would not end well. The officers come into the classroom during the halfway point of the academy's classes. "If you have struggled with what we have done so far, now is the time to leave. What we are going to do going forward will increase by 50%. So, if you think what we have done is hard, it will double as hard, starting today."

Not realizing what Zane had said Harper stood up to get something from the back of the room. Zane was puzzled as to why she was leaving. Several of the other students stood up to walk out. Harper's partner said, "I knew she couldn't cut it in a man's world."

Harper turned, "What are you talking about now Jenkins?"

"You are leaving the class, taking that walk of shame."

She looked directly at him. She responded, "You dumb-ass, I am getting something out of my bag. I am going to finish this class in three weeks. While kicking your ass every day. So shut the hell up." Kincade had a small smile on his face now that he knew she wasn't going anywhere.

"Okay, can I have everyone's attention? For the last three weeks you will work alone when we are in the field. Your times will no longer be given at the end of class. You will get your times one week before graduation. If you need to make improvements, you will have one week to get your times and grades up."

Jenkins turned to Harper, "Don't you ever talk to me like that again."

Harper responded, "Then stop talking to me and I will stop talking to you. It's exhausting to call you an ass every day."

Kincade slammed his hands down on the table. "If you two can't stop this childish mess, you both can pack your things and leave. I don't need this drama in my room." No longer partners Harper got her things and moved to another seat. Class continued without any more words exchanged. When the midday break came, Kincade asked for both of them to stay back after class.

"Look," Kincade started, "I am not sure what the problem is between the two of you. It needs to stop today."

Jenkins yelled, "If she continues to call me an ass, I will forget that she's a female and knock her ass out."

Harper responded, "Bring it."

"You both have been warned. I am not playing."

After the mid-day break, they were in the field, "Looking to your left you see week one, week two, and the exam. Everything you need to do to complete the program is on the field." Kincade explained. "You can only advance if you have a certain score, you will not know what is needed to pass until the last week." Harper ran her course like she always had. As class came to an end, there was a note on her bag. "Meet me at the parking garage on 12th & main street level 6."

Harper went to level 6. She parked next to Zane's car and he hopped into her car. "Let me explain about today."

Before he could start, she said, "No worries I know that you want to have that part of our day to stay business especially in front of others."

"I am glad you understand what is going on," Zane replied. "I would love to see you every day, I can't wait until graduation." They both laughed. Zane continued, "will you be okay, if we waited until we finished the program to go out again? It feels dirty sneaking around."

Harper interrupted him. "It's ok, it is only three weeks."

"It will be hard," Zane laughed.

Haper blushed at the inside joke. "Have you seen your grades? Are you not paying attention to your speed and agility."

She responded "No."

"Keep doing what you are doing, and you will be fine. For the next two weeks I need you to stay focused. Don't do anything different, also know that when I am looking at you, I am thinking of so many ways that we can go out."

Zane said he has been away from the office for a while, he needed to get back to the station. Harper said "Wait, before you leave how long has that car been there?" she points across the parking lot.

He responded "I don't remember if it was there when we got here or not. I didn't see it pull up while we were talking."

She says, "I feel creepy about it."

He tells her not to worry about it, gives her a kiss on the cheek. "This should hold you for a little bit," Harper blushes as she says good-bye.

When they pulled out of the parking garage, so did the car that was sitting in the lot with them. She memorized the plate number. The car began to follow her, *why is this car following me.* She ran a traffic light to lose him. As she walked into the house Andi could tell that she was visibly shaken. She told Andi what happened, "Do you want me to call Zane?"

"No, I don't want to get him upset if it all in my mind."

Harper got a glass of wine and took a long relaxing bath. While she relaxed, Zane texted Andi, "Hey, would you help me plan a graduation party for Harper?"

She responded, "I would love to."

"Don't worry about cost you can use my credit card to get what you need." Andi eyes widen as she read the message. "Do something, she would really like." Andi responded, "I am on it."

The next day Andi had a job to with just a little over a week to plan and execute this party.

While Andi was planning the party Harper was busy breaking records and making others mad. At the end of class, Zane pulled everyone together, "We are five days away from completion of the program. I am proud of you all for your efforts and dedication to this program. As it stands right now you all are on track to graduate. I want to warn you that you can still fail this class. This is no time to slack on your hard work. You also don't know your scores, there are five of you that are one point away from passing or failing. Fifteen of you are in the safety zone.

"Continue to push hard and don't let up and everyone will pass the program."

This was a hard day for Harper. She left without any eye contact with Zane. He yelled "St. James!" but she continued to walk out the door. When she returned home Andi, reminded her she only had four days to go, "If anyone can push through, it would be you."

To hear that made Harper feel encouraged, yet she was still feeling drained and uneasy. *Why is this car always around. What is it that they want.* She tried not to think about it, she took her shower and went to bed. 3:30 in the morning came fast. Andi looked in on Harper to make sure she was sleeping. Once she confirmed that she was Andi, sent a text to Zane, "Can we meet its urgent."

"Yes, that's not a problem, I can meet you in 20 minutes." Andi gathered her things and headed to the coffee shop down the street. As she was leaving, she noticed a car in the same description as what Harper described, now she was afraid to leave the house and leave Harper alone. She texted Zane to come to the house instead. It was urgent that he got to the house. When Zane arrived, he saw how shaken Andi was, "What is going on?"

She didn't have any choice but to tell him what was going on. "Over the last week Harper has told me about a car following her home. I think it started when you guys where in the parking garage." Zane had a strange look come over his face.

"Wait what? She said something about a car when we were talking, and I shrugged it off." Andi said, "It's been happening for a few days now." He told Andi not to worry about it, he would put his detective on finding out who was behind this.

"We are four days away from graduation, don't worry I will take care of this, and you work on the party." Harper's bedroom door opened, as she was getting ready for class. Zane quickly ran out the front door, he ducked behind a car as Andi waved goodbye to him. As she walked down the stairs Andi said that everything was going to be okay. "Stay focused and these days will go by quickly. I promise you."

Harper finished the week strong. She left Friday again with no eye contact with Zane and ignoring Jenkins, Jenkins turned to Zane, "What's up with her?"

Zane looked at Jenkins, *is showing signs of being concerned. Why is he not giving her shit like he usually does.* That didn't sit well with him.

Now that the weekend was there, Harper was out grocery shopping. That uneasy feeling came over her again. As she shopped, she felt like someone was following her, but when she turned around no one was there. She was starting to get very anxious; the store was starting to spin. She was about to pass out when she heard a deep voice, "Harper."

When she turned, she saw it was Zane and collapsed in his chest. When she came too, he asked her, "What happened?"

She began to cry and tell him everything that had been going on over the last week or so. "Someone in here is following me."

"Let's get you home."

Andi came out of her room when she heard them come in.

"Oh, my goodness what happened?" Zane began to tell her what happened at the store. Now she was worried, "What are we going to? My husband will be here in time for graduation. When he arrives, I can go over everything with him to help keep her safe."

"Stop it! Stop it! I am right here in the room," Harper yelled. "No one has to do anything. I just got worked up about someone or I thought someone was following me and I just passed out. Next week is graduation and I need to be prepared for it."

Zane told harper he was here for her and wanted her to be safe. He cared a lot about her. He would be crushed if something happened to her. With his statement Harper knew she wanted to get to know him better. "I promise I will stay in the house until it is time to return to the precinct." That was the answer that he wanted to hear.

Out of nowhere, Harper said, "You are welcome to stay the weekend if you like. The sofa is very comfortable," Andi agreed.

"If I stay the weekend, I may never leave." Everyone in the room started to laugh; "I need you to go lay down please." Zane didn't leave until Harper was asleep. He told Andi he would be back after he got his clothes. He would be in and out of the house to keep an eye on both ladies. "We also can finalize the party while she is sleeping."

Andi worked hard to keep Harper calm. Zane also was there to help with keeping her mind off what was going on outside. Since the grocery store trip, the car had not been outside. The weekend was starting to come to an end, Harper prepared for Monday. 3:30 came fast.

At the precinct Zane gave his last instructions for the program. "On Friday, most, if not all of you, will graduate. You will receive an envelope; in it you will get your final grade. Also, you will get your precinct location. Most importantly, you will get your badge." Everyone was excited, "Ok calm down, here's how the week will look.

"Monday through Wednesday will go as follows: Monday is your last full class. Tuesday is the final test; you will get your physicals done at that time. Wednesday- you will get fitted for your formal dress uniforms. You will need them from time to time. Stay focused on the next 30 hours. We have a few people still on the edge of going either way."

The class took the last field test, but Harper was not focused on the task at hand. When the whistle blew, she changed clothes. She was proud that she had pushed through everything, and it was now over. She called an Uber to keep the person following her sitting in the car.

This was time to relax, with all the stress she was under, looking forward to Friday was all she could think about. Harper walked into her house; she could smell something amazing coming from the kitchen. She knew Andi couldn't cook, so it had to be only one person. She walked into the kitchen, and she was correct. It was Mike, Andi's husband. He had cooked a feast. So excited to see him, she almost knocked over the food on the counter. "I am so happy to see you and that you are back safely." He asked how she was doing, because Andi had kept him up to date on everything that was happening here.

Harper responds, "I'm holding up. Just waiting for graduation to be over and start my vision." She looked at the table, "Why are there four places set for dinner?"

At that moment, the doorbell rang, Mike asked Harper to get the door. When she opened the door, there stood Zane. Her eyes widened as well as her smile. Before he could say hello, she hugged him like she hadn't seen him in a year. She looked up and she whispered in his ear. "Don't turn around but the black car is back. Black tinted windows, 2021 sedan, when I let, you go turn to pick the mail off the steps."

When Zane turned to do as Harper asked the car drove off. He went inside to spend the evening with her and the crew. The evening was going great, Harper told them to continue to enjoy themselves, but she needed to lay down. She looked at Zane and thanked him for everything. Zane said, "You are not getting away that easily." He walked her to her room. He explained that after what just happened, he was not leaving. He was staying until after graduation or longer if this wasn't figured out, "I will sleep on the sofa."

Harper didn't disagree with his plan. "How are going to get back and forth to the station without anyone noticing that we came to work together?"

"I have someone that will meet us a block away to drop you off while I park my car." This plan went on for two days. It seemed to be working, the black car had not been seen since Zane started staying there.

Zane, and the other officers entered the room, "Good Morning, everyone. We will call you up one by one. You are not allowed to open your envelope until instructed."

Everyone got an envelope along with a gym bag with their names on it. Zane followed up with, "Does everyone have an envelope?"

The room yelled, "Yes!"

Zane asked the room to look at the screen, "here you will see the top three students. 1) St. James was top student 2) Jenkins-second 3) Rogers was third. The room erupted in cheer. Jenkins turned to Haper, he gave her a hug, "Good job partner."

The announcements continued, "St. James and Jenkins will be your speakers at graduation. Rogers will speak on his experience with the program and you two will follow. We will start tomorrow at 8:00am sharp and will end at 10:00am sharp. We have room for 300 people at the event. We will turn people away if needed. Okay open your envelopes, this will tell you where you will be stationed. Now go enjoy the rest of your day, don't be late tomorrow."

Harper was so excited she didn't care if there was a car following them or not. All she wanted was a hot shower and to go to bed early, "I can't wait until tomorrow."

The day Harper had been waiting for was here. She had on a dark navy blue two-piece outfit with her hair pulled back in a tight bun. Everyone was in the gym; the crowd was very large. After she and Jenkins told an amused crowd, how they didn't get along, yet happy to be standing with each other talking to them, Harper gave Jenkins a big hug. She thanked him for pushing her. He also thanked her. The ceremony was underway, everyone got a lapel pin along with their badge. St. James was now an official Private Investigator.

Zane took the mic to inform every one of the location for the graduation party. Please join us at 11:00am to celebrate and have breakfast. Andi told Harper she would meet them there. She needed to change her shoes, she forgot to bring an extra pair. She was really heading over to the event to make sure that everything was set up and ready to go. She didn't plan for the number of people that Zane had invited but what she didn't know he had the caterer double the food, she had nothing to worry about.

Once there, the place looked amazing. There was a table set up for each graduate to make sure that they felt included. Andi turned to her husband, "I can't wait for Harper to see this. She is going to love it."

Harper was still at the precinct's gym. She made eye contact with Zane and gave a nod that she was okay and would see him in a few. Harper now was in street clothes and was heading out the door. She was heading to the parking garage, that uneasy feeling was no longer there. As she entered the parking garage people were leaving to head over to the party, Harper was waving at people as they left the garage.

"Harper St. James, I thought I would never catch up with you."

Harper turned. "What are you doing here? I thought you were gone. What do you want I have a party to go to." People walking by paid no attention to the conversation.

"I am back for a reason, and you will hear what I have to say."

Harper responded, "No, I don't have to hear anything you have to say. I have a party to attend to."

"Do you really?"

Andi and Zane were waiting for Harper to walk through the door, the party had started 30 minutes ago. *Where could she be* they both were wondering. Harper's classmates were also now looking for her. They wanted to take a group photo. As Zane was reaching for his phone, a message was on his phone. "Get to the parking garage NOW!"

Zane and fellow officers got to the parking garage, there was Harper's new gym bag on the ground, car keys and phone next to it. Everyone stopped, there was a burning SUV next to the car.

Someone yelled, "Call Hill and Bates to the parking garage NOW!"

POLICE SUMMARY REPORT

"Hill and Bates! You are needed at the parking garage on the third floor. You got a burning SUV and a new P.I. missing."

"Oh shit!" Bates yelled.

They ran to the door yelling, "Pull that garage footage now." They were out of breath once they got to the parking garage.

The section with Harper's car was blocked off, Zane was struggling with not showing emotions. Hill and Bates were yelling, "What's happening Kincade?"

"Once of our graduates didn't show for her celebrations."

Hill interrupted, "Her?"

"Yes St. James never made it to the party. When we were all leaving the gym, she said she was on her way. She was right behind us when we were leaving. She wanted to change her shoes. So, we went ahead."

"Is there anything you can tell us? Was she acting strange?"

Zane said, "Yes, she felt like someone was following her. We wrote it off as exhaustion and nerves from the program coming to an end."

Standing at the caution tape were her classmates. When the message went out to Zane, it was in a group chat in error. Along with the classmates stood Andi and her husband. Andi was demanding that she be let in pass the caution tape. They let her pass, but Mike had to stay behind the tape.

"Any idea why someone would follow her or want to harm her?"

"No clue," Andi responded. "This didn't start until she began the program. It was more obvious the last few weeks that someone was following her."

"Thank you," Bates, said and turned to Hill, "let's go back to the office while they get more information."

So now it looks like we have a pattern on our hands.

1) four women are missing, near their home, car or place of employment.
2) Their phones and personal items all are left behind.
3) Issues with the surveillance camera, this one we are still waiting on.
4) It seems like they knew the person in question.
5) The biggest thing is that dam burning SUV. I think we need to figure out what these women have in common. What does the burning SUV on fire mean? We need the answers to that question before it happens again.

"Bring in the family members of all those that have gone missing. Let's see if we can get any ideas if they know each other. Also, we can find insight on the toy SUV. We need to figure this out before another person goes missing."

5

DINA

Standing at the edge of the cliff staring at an empty shell of a car wondering where he went, Dina fell to the ground. She was devastated that he was gone, or was he dead? What happened to him? She was crying asking what would happen to her now.

As the months passed, Dina did nothing but stay in bed. Everything that her and Justice worked hard to build together was now in jeopardy. All of the money was gone, the business was set to close at the end of the month.

Dina was facing eviction; she was facing hard times and nowhere to turn. One of her friends came over to check on her, to find her sitting in the dark with tears in her eyes. As he began to open the windows to let in the sunlight, she was not ready to leave the house. She looked at him, "What am I going to do?"

He suggested that she start an online business, since she was not ready to leave the house. Dina said she would think about it, but she was feeling bad. Chauncey thought she was depressed. She became very ill so he took her to the doctor. After an hour in the office, Dina came out with a shocked look on her face. Chauncey asked, "What is wrong with you? You are not dying, are you?"

She flopped down in the chair beside him, still not talking. She took a deep breath, turned to Chauncey, "I am pregnant."

For a moment they were happy then sad again. "What's wrong?"

"Justice will never see his child." She got home safe, and Dina said she needed to change her life for the better. There was a church that she walked past every Sunday. Maybe this Sunday she would stop in. She made a list of things she wanted to do in life. Her number one goal was to be happy.

The next Sunday she reached the stairs that she would sit on to listen to the service. This time she was going to find the nerve to walk inside. This was what she needed. During the service the preacher asked if there was anyone that was new to the church, if so to please join him at the front of the church.

Dina got up and walked to the front of the church. He asked everyone what brought them to the church today. When they got to Dina, "I need a change in my life. I need a purpose. I want to be a better person."

"Amen! Would you be open to meet a mentor after church services to help you reach your goals?" She nodded and returned to her seat. When church was over, she made her way to the front of the church, the preacher asked her to take a seat while he located her mentor. The Decan came out, sat next to her, "tell me what's going on. I am Decan Raines how can the church help you?" The preacher, the Decan and Dina worked together to get a plan for her.

She told of the story of Justice, the loss of business and how she was pregnant. He said that he understood what was going on and he could help her get to a better place in life. Dina left the church with a newfound energy. Once home she looked over the list of things she needed to start working on.

She began to set up her online business and the church helped her with her rent and bills for the next three months. This would help her work on getting her "Styles by D" up and running. A few days later she received a text asking her how she was doing with the list of things to do. As she was responding to the preacher, there was a knock on the door. It was the Decan.

She invited him in. "Nice home, Dina."

"Thank you," she replied.

"Small but it all mine. I will have to look for another place to live once the baby is born. I can't have him or her sleeping in one of my dresser drawers." A small chuckle came out.

"So, tell me how have you been doing? How are things going with you and the list? I have done a few things off the list since Sunday. I got a text from the preacher a few minutes ago. I was just about to tell him how I was doing. Is it ok if I call and talk to you both at the same time?

"Yes, please do."

She called the preacher and put him on speaker. "I want to thank you both," she said, "I have implemented a few of the items on my list. I have cleaned my apartment, gone grocery shopping and I set up my online clothing business. In doing these things, I have noticed that I am in a very good mood. Since leaving the church things I thought to be bad or would bring me down, but it wasn't that bad after all. It is a message or a learning tool that is being provided for me. Not everything that is bad is meant to break you."

The Decan was happy with her progress. "Remember on Sunday you will get a new set of things to work on. Each week they will get harder and harder, but they are to make you stronger. Next Sunday you will be paired with one of our female church members as well. We want you to have all of the church services at your disposal.

Dina thanked both with tears rolling down her cheeks.

"One last question, when can we expect your little bundle of Joy?"

"I'm roughly five months along."

"That is great," he said as he wrote that in his book.

"Thank you for the visit today. I will let our ladies of the church know you are close to delivery, so that they can plan a little something for you."

Sunday was here, Dina had finished her list and was looking forward to her new one. As she got to the church stairs, she had a feeling come over her. She couldn't say what it was, but it just didn't feel right. She stopped at the church doors unable to move. One of the church members saw her and offered some assistance through the door. The choir was singing a joyful sound filled the building. She made eye contact with the Decan; he gave her a nod and she took her seat.

"Welcome everyone," the preacher said. "Today is a special day. Little Ricado has decided to dedicate his life to the lord. Is there anyone who would like to join him today in his quest?" Slowly people began to stand. Something came over Dina, she slowly stood up and walked to the front of the church.

At that moment she could feel the love and support from the church, compared to what she experienced prior to being a part of the church. The Decan was helping Dina with her weekly assignments. People in the church started to talk about how they were spending a lot of time together. Not knowing that the Decan was assigned to her from the preacher, along with a lady that taught Sunday school.

Dina had goals she wanted to meet, and a little church gossip would not stop her from reaching them. A week away from the dedication of herself to the church, she was feeling excited, but there was something not right. She told the Deacon when she leaves the church, it feels like someone is behind her when she is walking home. She has been writing it off because she was pregnant.

He told her that if it continued to bother her let him know and he would walk or take her home. He told her that she meant a lot to him. She smiled with no response.

Dina was preparing for her baptism. "It is your turn," the preacher said. And first, the Deacon said a few powerful and heartfelt words, then they dipped her back. When she appeared, the Deacon was waiting for her bended knee.

He told her that he knew this moved fast, but God made no mistakes, and he was following his heart. He respected her for all she had gone through and would love for her and her baby to join his family.

She responded, "I would love to, but are you sure?"

He assured her that he was, and his kids would love her as much as he did. A few minutes passed, everyone was watching and waiting for her answer. She took a deep breath, looked at the preacher who was smiling, she looked back at the Deacon dripping wet from the baptism, "Yes, yes, I will marry you."

Some of the church members were happy, others whispered as they walked past. Saying mean things like, "I hope she doesn't wear white," "he knows his kids will not like her." "I hope they don't move in together until after they are married." Dina heard everything, the good comments as well as the mean ones. Once outside, she told him that they might be making a mistake by getting married. The church doesn't seem to approve. He said it is not their place to approve or disapprove. He said they will take all the proper steps to make sure they are doing the right thing.

Dina felt better about her decision. She told him while going through counseling and meeting with his children she would stay in her apartment until they were married.

He agreed. He was happy that she hadn't changed her mind. Over the next few months, they went to couple's classes at the church, along with family classes to help his kids get used to Dina and the idea of her and a baby moving into the house with them. Those classes were the hardest, she had to get the kids to understand she wasn't there to take their mother's place. She just wanted to be a part of their lives. She told the kids that she would do everything she could to help them remember her, not to forget her.

The children began to call her M.D., short for momma Dina. They started to get excited about a new brother or sister. Following one of the family meetings the kids showed Dina how they had painted the room with bunnies on the wall. She was so happy that they did that, and she began to cry. The kids thought she was upset, but soon found out that it was tears of joy.

Dina stood up to hug them, a sharp pain came over her back. She fell back in the chair. They rushed to her side, "Are you ok?"

She said, "Yes, I am having pains in my back and my stomach." The preacher said she was in labor, "Let's get her to the hospital." They got her to the hospital quickly, while they were waiting for the baby to make an appearance, she thought she saw someone at the door.

She asked the kids, "Did you see who that was at the door?" Everyone was looking at each other like they didn't know what she was talking about. Her pains started to worsen; the first lady of the church took the kids out in the waiting room. Dina was about to say something when a pain hit her, then there was blood all over the bed and she was rushed out of the room into surgery.

The church congregation soon gathered in the waiting room, saying prayers, and singing. Three hours later, the Deacon appeared, "Everything is ok, both are doing fine. She had a beautiful baby girl. If you want to see her and the baby, they will be in the room within the hour. We can have four or five back at time for 10 minutes. Thank you all for being here and supporting her during this difficult time. It means a lot to our family."

Someone in the waiting room asked, "what is her name?"

"She named her Justine."

"How sweet," the group echoed. Dina picked that name because it would have parts of her father's name. Dina stayed in the hospital for two weeks, because of the difficulty she had along with getting an infection. The doctors thought it would be in the best interests of them both to stay to have the best support. The Deacon came by to pick up her and Justine. On the way home Dina told him that while she was there, on several occasions, she thought she saw someone standing in the doorway with all black on.

She asked the nurses if they saw anyone, but no one could confirm if they did or didn't see who she was talking about. One nurse said it could be the pain medication that had her seeing things. It was common to see things while on that strong of medication. It was really bothering her, something she had a hard time shaking.

At her apartment, Dina began to plan her little backyard wedding. She was working on moving her stuff into the house and getting her online store up and running. She had set a date for two months away. She wanted to have a fun backyard cook-out style wedding. No one had to dress up, they were just there to support the union and have fun.

She had completed the planning of the wedding, now it was time to start packing up her apartment. Her goal was not to have a lot of stuff to take to the house in two months. The preacher offered his storage shed for her to use until she moved in. The church didn't want her to have to do all of the packing alone, the men and women of the church arrived at her apartment with boxes, tape, and all the moving supplies she would need along with a moving truck to take the boxes to storage.

The ladies of the church were watching the baby. Dina asked, "Did you lovely ladies come here to help pack, or did you come to play with Justine?" They all said at the same time, "We came to play with the baby."

So far, Dina had ten boxes ready to go and was working on a few more. Her back was starting to hurt, she didn't want to push it too much.

Everyone had arrived to help. Boxes were going out the door. It occurred to Dina that this was really happening. While at the van, she was telling the men how to pack the truck. The Deacon noticed her holding her back. "Why don't you sit down, we will get the truck packed."

"Ok," she said, "I will take a break."

"We are going to get another load I want you to sit here and not move." She was sitting in the van waiting for them to return, a large box was heading towards the truck, when she got out to tell them where to put it.

She was looking at the box, "I don't remember having that box in the apartment."

"We will make space for it, that box needs to go all the way to the back of the truck," a muffled voice replied.

"Okay." Dina walked in front of the person with the large box and pointed to the back, "you can put that all the way to the back, preacher." The box was dropped to the ground, and everyone heard glass breaking.

Dina turned, "Are you ok?" As she turned, she took a few steps back in shock. She yelled, "What are you doing here? How did you know where I was?" There was no reply, "What is wrong with you? You never had a hard time finding words in the past.

The Deacon and preacher returned with boxes; they thought Dina was in the back of the truck. So, they proceeded to the back of the truck. That was when they didn't see her back there but on the ground was a burning SUV. They started yelling for Dina. The first lady came out to see what was going on. She was carrying the baby; she walked around the side of the truck and there was a box of clothes strewn on the ground. The first lady yelled, "What is this what is going on?"

They yelled back at her to call 911 and hurry because Dina was gone.

POLICE SUMMARY REPORT

"911 how can we help you? Please slow down a burning what? Not again, someone will be there right away. Don't touch a thing."

Dispatch called to the back, "Hill and Bates get up here NOW!"

"What's up, you know we are working on that case."

"You might want to press hold."

"Why what now?"

"I just got a call you have another burning toy SUV."

"Hell No!" Bates said.

"Hell, yes," the dispatch yelled back. Hill yelled back to several people, "Let's go, we have another SUV."

Hill and Bates arrived greeted by the upset deacon, "please tell us what happened."

"We were in the process of moving my fiancé'. Her back started to hurt, and I asked her to sit down while we went back upstairs to get more boxes. When we returned, she was gone, the box of clothes thrown on the ground. these clothes are not hers, and then there is this burning toy."

Bates asked, "Do you know how long you were gone?"

"I think we were gone fifteen to twenty minutes."

"Where was she when you left?"

"She was sitting in the truck on the passenger's side doing something on her cellphone."

"Is her cellphone still here?"

"No, it is not," the Deacon replied.

Bates yelled to Hill to come over quickly. Hill gets over to them, "what's up?"

"Her cellphone is not here."

"What did you say?"

"Her cellphone is not here!"

They both turned to the deacon, with hope in their eyes. Hill asked, Do you have the 360 locator on her phone?"

The Deacon pulled out his phone, "I am not sure what you are looking for, here's my phone."

They opened his phone, and there it was the 360-location application. Everyone jumped in the police car and took off. The Deacon yelled, "Wait what's happening?"

One of the police officers that stayed behind told him, "I think you just saved her life."

6
WE GOT YOU!

Police cars were speeding through the city. Bates was driving and Hill was following the 360-application telling which direction to go. "Oh Shit!"

"What's wrong now?"

"The location has stopped. It's gone."

"What is the last location shown on the phone?"

"It is in a downtown warehouse. It is in the warehouse district. The 360 shows it is going in circles in this one building."

Bates said, "Let's go to that one."

A car pulled up to the back of a warehouse. Dina was dragged out of the car and pushed into the warehouse. As she was walking through the warehouse, it looked like an old meat packing plant. The person in black opened the door and pushed Dina inside the room, once inside Dina couldn't believe her eyes.

There was Reya, Kourtney, Lyssa, and Harper chained to poles in the middle of the room.

"Wait is that, Justice? Is that him tied to the chair? I thought he was dead." Dina was pushed to one of the poles, on the pole was her name. first her feet then her arms, and her mouth covered in duct tape. Once chained to the pole she pulls off the duct tape.

"I hate you all," the person in black slowly turned around, it was Cecily. She had been friends with Justice for years. Their friendship was like no other. It was not romantic; they had a strong bond. She trusted him and he trusted her with everything. "Who was with you when all the winches left you? Me! I was the one that was there when everything that could go wrong did go wrong. Instead, you of reaching out to me you pushed me away."

Outside you could hear sirens blaring, they were getting closer. "Do you know why you went off the road?" She yelled as she slapped Justice in the face. "I did it, in a moment of rage I wanted to see you suffer and everyone that was near you." While she continued to talk, he realized that his ropes were not tied. Not everyone in the room had chains.

You could hear the police getting closer to where they were. Cecily turned to address each woman. As she walked past each one, she rubbed a gun along their faces. She stopped at Harper, she stared at her with such hatred. Harper looked at her, "What did I do to you? I don't even know who you are." Harper continued, "If anything I should feel hatred towards you. At this point I only feel pity."

Cecily put the gun in Harper's mouth to shut her up. "He loved you. It was the love I always wanted from him. The smile that came to his face when he talks about you, I wanted that!"

When Harper tried to respond she still had the gun in her mouth. "You were the one he wanted which makes you the first to die. I want him to sit here and watch me kill every one of you one by one. Dina yelled, "The police will find us before you can do that."

There was aloud pop, silencing Dina. Cecily shot her.

"Who's next to challenge my plan? I will take you out also."

Reya yelled, "How did you find us? Why are you doing this? We did nothing to you."

"Stop with all the questions! I followed Justice from the gym that night knowing that he would travel a curvy road. I had cut his brakes earlier and I wanted to watch this happen in person. I was not expecting all of you to show up, that's when I decided that you all need to pay for the pain that I was feeling.

"Then there was nobody, I was driving down the highway, I saw Justice walking down the highway, so I decided to drive slowly on the shoulder of the highway. Justice went into the woods, that's when I got off the highway."

Cecily started to walk in Reya's direction, "I saw you taking Justice back to your apartment. So, I followed you, it was not my intention to harm you, but you got in the way." She placed the gun in Reya's mouth. "When you both would leave your apartment, I would go in, and I got all the information that you collected. That made it very easy for me to take care of my plan.

"Thanks for making this so easy for me. I took photos of the wall and then the rest was history."

Kourtney began to cry. "Shut up! I am sick of all this crying."

At that moment Justice lunged at Cecily, knocking her to the ground. The gun slid in front of Harper's feet. While Cecily was on the ground, Harper was able to work her hands free.

Justice and Cecily were rolling on the floor, Harper tok the ropes away from her feet. She grabbed the gun. She fired it in the air and everyone stopped moving. Cecily was looking at Justice, "All I ever wanted you to do was to love me like you loved her. I gave you 8 years of my life. And in return I got nothing."

Suddenly, the doors are kicked open by the police. They are yelling for Harper to put the gun down. Cecily told Justice, "If you are not going to love me the way I want you too, you will not love anyone else." She reached for a gun that was on her side and pointed it at his head.

Harper screamed, which distracted Cecily. Justice took the gun and was then standing over Cecily with the gun pointed at her. The police yelled to drop the gun.

"Put it down on the ground!"

As justice was about to put the gun down, Cecily grabbed it, pulling Justice down with it. She was getting ready to shoot Justice. The police yelled again and the gun went off. Both Cecily and Justice were lying on the floor covered in blood.

Harper screamed "Noooooooooooo!"

The police were getting the women free not realizing that Dina was dead. They took the chains off her, and she fell to the floor. The police radioed for the EMTs to come in with multiple stretchers. They were taking the women out one at a time. Still lying on the ground was Cecily and Justice.

Harper was leaning over them over them crying as Justice started to move. She screamed for the EMTs to come over. Once they got him up on the stretcher, they realized Cecily was dead.

The last people to come out of the warehouse was Justice and Harper along with the police. Justice was screaming, "Why do you have me in handcuffs? I didn't do anything wrong. It was that crazy bitch that is dead back there. She killed Dina and tried to kill me."

At that moment the Deacon heard what he said and rushed to the police for answers. The deacon turned to Justice; "I will make sure you never see Justine a day in your life."

Who is Justine he wondered but went back to trying to get out of the cuffs. Bates was talking to Justice, "You have the right to remain silent."

Justice was still yelling that he did nothing wrong. Bates, "Shut up you are charged with murder, attempted murder on four counts, and hindering a police investigation. There is no way you are going to get away with this it's too many people who seen you."

146

As they put Justice in the rescue squad, the women lined up and watched him drive away. Harper looked at the ladies, "I know this is not over!"

EPILOGUE

There was a loud buzzer and the door opened. In walked Justice in an orange and white jumpsuit. He sat down staring through the glass. Then he picked up the phone. On the other side of the glass was Harper.

He was happy to see her but that didn't last long. "Don't smile," Harper said. "I am here to tell you how much I dislike you for everything you have done to me and the others. Now you have one dead on your hands."

Justice responded, "I did that for you. I never wanted anything to happen to you. I have always loved you. I just didn't know how to love you."

"Please stop talking," Harper said. "You never wanted a relationship and you wanted to make sure I never had one. Let me explain the damage that you have caused.

"Reya is now in a mental hospital. Lysa is selling her business, she has plans to move out of the country. Kourtney has disappeared.

Dina is dead and leaves behind your daughter. Yes, you have a child, one you will never see."

Justice looked at harper with tears in his eyes, "What about you?"

"What about me?" Harper stared back at him. "I am good, and I plan to stay that way. I am now part of the police department. I am going to say this one time, we have some unfinished business. You destroyed my life twice. Every time I rebuild it you somehow manage to tear it down.

"Now it's my turn to tear your life down. You will get three to four years to wonder just how I am going to do it. When you walk out of this jail, I will be somewhere very close. So, I would watch your back at every turn."

Harper slammed down the phone and turned to walk out as Justice remained seated. She let the officer know she was leaving. They grabbed Justice by the arm, but he started to resist. They kicked his legs out from under him as they dragged him out of the room. Harper watched as the door slammed behind him. You could hear him screaming.

"Harper try your best to take me down. I will see you rot in Hell before I let you do this. Go to hell Harper!"